THE
SINGING
JEWEL

Dumarest watched the jewel cupped in Marta's hands. It had gained an inner luminescence as, triggered by the heat of flesh, it responded in vibrant light and sound. The glow became brighter, splintered in a sudden mass of broken rainbows which filled starship's salon with drifting color, a brilliance which gave everything an enticing magic. Of them all Marta was the most transfigured.

She stood like a priestess of some esoteric cult, hands uplifted, the effulgence of the jewel bathing her uplifted face and robbing it of the scars of time. The light gave her beauty and she drank it and returned it.

Imperious in its demand for attention was the song of the jewel itself. It lifted, keening, undulating, a note of crystalline purity . . . a song without words but one which held love and hope and joy and all the promise there ever could be and the happiness ever imagined. . . .

WEB
OF
SAND

E. C. Tubb

DAW BOOKS, INC.
DONALD A. WOLLHEIM, PUBLISHER
New York

For Ethel Lindsay

FIRST PRINTING, JULY 1979

1 2 3 4 5 6 7 8 9

 DAW TRADEMARK REGISTERED
U.S. PAT. OFF. MARCA
REGISTRADA. HECHO EN U.S.A.

PRINTED IN U.S.A.

Chapter One

Marta Caine had a singing jewel which she took from its box and held cupped in her palms as she stood in the salon of the *Urusha*.

"From Necho," she said, her eyes on the crystal. "I bought it when young and have carried it with me ever since. A long time now. Too long."

"It looks dull," said Kemmer. "Dead."

"It's fatigued."

"Why haven't we seen it before?" Grish Mettalus leaned forward from where he stood behind Chai Teoh. Like the girl, he was tall, slim, eyes slanted beneath narrow brows but where her face held a high-boned delicacy his features bore a broad and flattened stamp. "You are unkind, Marta. The gem would have helped relieve our boredom."

"As I said, it is tired." The veined hands seemed to press reassuringly against the crystal cupped in the palms. "I have kept it cooped in darkness too long. When we reach Fendris I shall set it on a high and open place where it can feed on sunlight and starlight, be caressed by soft breezes and laved with gentle rains. Then it will regain its vitality and become young again." Bitterness edged her voice. "Would to God that it was as easy for others to restore their beauty."

"You are beautiful enough," said Kemmer with heavy gallantry. "With a warmth no stone can possess."

"You are kind to say so, Maurice—but my mirror tells a different story."

"Mirrors can lie. The beauty of a woman is more than a patina of skin. It is the need within her, the spirit, the response she creates in those who watch her walk and talk and smile. A thing of the heart. Am I not right, Earl?"

Dumarest nodded, making no comment as he watched the jewel cupped in the woman's hands. It no longer looked gray and dull like flawed glass but had gained an inner luminescence as, triggered by the metabolic heat and stimulation of flesh, it responded in vibrant light and sound. The glow became brighter, splintered in a sudden mass of broken rainbows which filled the salon with swaths of drifting color, a kaleidoscopic brilliance which gave the chairs, the tables and fittings a transient and enticing magic. And as with the furnishings so those who stood bathed in the splendor now streaming from the jewel; Kemmer, suddenly no longer the gross trader he was but now a figure of dignity as the harsh and somber shape of Carl Santis the mercenary took on hints of a chivalry he had never known from a tradition he had never suspected. Mettalus, the girl standing before him, Dumarest who now wore a shattered spectrum to decorate his face and hair and clothing. But of them all Marta was the most transfigured.

She stood like a priestess of some esoteric cult, hands lifted now, the effulgence of the jewel bathing her uplifted face and robbing it of the scars and marks of time. The skin had smoothed, the mesh of lines marring the flesh at the corners of the eyes lost in flattering glows. The lips had gained fullness, the chin liberated from sagging tissue, the bones of cheeks prominent above exotic concavities. The nose had thinned, become arrogant in haughty affirmation of youthful pride, age and dissolution stripped away to show the girl she once had been. The hair, too, had changed, now displaying glints and glimmers of vibrant hues, of sheens and enticing softness.

The light gave her beauty and she drank it and returned it through the touch of her hands, the emitted nervous tensions of her body which stimulated the symbiote she held into a higher plane of existence.

Chai Teoh gasped as it began to sing. "Grish! What—"

"Be silent, girl!" Santis rasped the command. "Be still!"

His tone held the snap of one accustomed to obedience, but more imperious in its demand for attention was the song of the jewel itself. It lifted, keening, undulating, a note of crystalline purity which penetrated skin and bone and muscle to impact on the nerves and brain and the raw stuff of emotion itself. A song without words and without a predictable pattern but one which held love and hope and joy and all the promise there ever could be and all the happiness ever imagined.

"God!" Kemmer's whisper was a prayer as he stood, tears streaming over his rounded cheeks. "God—dear God!"

A man lost in the past or dreaming of what he had known or touched by a gentleness hitherto unsuspected and frightening in its overwhelming tenderness. He did not weep alone. The face of Chai Teoh glistened with moist color, shimmering pearls falling unheeded from the line of her jaw as she stood lost in a radiant pleasure. As Santis stood, his scarred face a prison for his eyes, the eyes wells of somber introspection.

Mettalus said, "This is fantastic! I've never—"

"Be silent!" snapped the mercenary. "Hold your tongue!"

His scowl deepened as the singing faltered and then, reluctantly, faded to quaver and finally to cease leaving a silence so intense that it could almost be felt as a tangible presence. As the sound died so the shimmering colors diminished, closing in to form a luminescent cloud, a ball, a tinge on the surface of the crystal, a memory.

For a long moment Marta Caine held her poise then, slowly, she lowered her hands to stand looking at the dull surface of the gem. Robbed of its magic she looked as she was, a woman too old for comfort, one who had lived hard and who showed it. The face, lax, showed the marks of cheap cosmetic surgery; subtle distortions of ill-matched implants giving her a pathetically clownish appearance. Her hair looked like the graft it was. Her eyes when she finally raised her head, betrayed her misery.

For a moment only and then the mask reappeared, the hard cynicism which was her defense against misfortune and her shield against derision.

"Well? Did you like it?"

"It was superb!! Chai Teoh dabbed at her eyes. "So wonderful! I felt as if—oh, how can I explain?"

Grish Mettalus was direct. "How much?"

"For what?"

"For the jewel, of course, what else? I want it. How much?"

"It isn't for sale."

"And if it were I would buy it," said Kemmer. "Marta, you have been most gracious. I think I speak on behalf of us all when I thank you for having let us share the pleasure given by your jewel. From Necho, you say?"

"Yes."

"Necho." Kemmer pursed his lips. "A long way from here

but, perhaps, not too far if a high profit is to be made. Your home world?"

"No." Gently she restored the jewel to its box. "I was born on Lurus. My people owned a farm but the climate changed and what was once fertile ground turned into desert. A solar imbalance—" She shrugged. "The details are of no importance. I was young and decided to help as best I could. I traveled—it's an old story."

And one printed on her face. The mercenary said, "Did you ever return?"

"Does anyone?" The lid snapped shut on the box. "Did you?"

"No."

"Nor I," said Kemmer. "How about you, Earl?" He smiled as Dumarest shook his head. "Once we leave the nest it quickly loses its attraction. Sometimes we choose to dream of a childhood more pleasant than it really was and of a life garnished with false tinsel, but when it comes to it who would go back home if given the chance?" He shrugged, not waiting for an answer. "Well, how now to pass the time? Some cards?"

The *Urusha* was a small vessel, a free-trader plying on the edge of the Rift, and the passengers were left to entertain themselves. No real hardship with planets close and quicktime turning weeks into days, the drug slowing the metabolism and relieving the tedium of the journey. But even so boredom was an enemy and one to be combatted. Grish Mettalus had found his own method, making it plain he regarded Chai Teoh as his personal property and she, for reasons of her own, had not objected.

Marta grunted as they left the salon. "The girl's a fool. She is selling herself too cheaply."

"How can you know that?" Kemmer dealt cards and turned one over. "A jester. Match, beat or defer?" He watched as they made their bets, small amounts as to whether their own cards could show a value equal, higher or lower than the one exposed. A variant of High, Low, Man-In-Between. "You win, Carl. Well?" He looked at the woman. "How do you know?"

"I've ears. He paid her passage and has promised her an apartment on Fendris. Promises!" She echoed her contempt.

"So they come to nothing," said the trader. "But she has still earned passage."

"And could gain more." Santis scowled at his card lying face down on the table. "A settlement, perhaps. Even marriage. On a journey like this a girl could make a man her own. Mettalus is young and impressionable despite his cultivated air of sophisticated indifference, and the girl has charm."

"But no brains." Marta thinned her lips as, again, she lost. "And you're mistaken about Mettalus. He's older than he seems. Right, Earl?"

"I wouldn't know."

"Don't lie to me. You'd know and so would you, Carl, if you took the trouble to look. I can spot it—the way he stands, moves, walks. The way he acts. Young? He's old enough to be her father!"

"And so would make a better prize." Kemmer smiled as he dealt a new round. "There is no fool like an old fool and I speak from experience. But what are a few years between lovers? Age brings experience and a certain degree of tolerance. Matched to youth it can have a beneficial effect. Some cultures realize that. On Richemann, for example, no girl is permitted to marry a man less than twenty years older than herself and no man a woman less than twenty years younger. That way all gain the benefit of both worlds; when young you match with age, when old you enjoy youth. Sometimes I think I will settle there."

"Why don't you?"

"The journey is long and I not too fond of unripe fruit."

"You degenerate swine!" Her words were hard but she smiled as she spoke them and Dumarest knew she was joking. Knew too that she and the trader had both found comfort in each other's arms.

He said, "Have any of you made this journey before?"

"From Elgish to Fendris?" Kemmer shook his head. "Marta? How about you, Carl?"

"Once—some time ago now." The mercenary frowned, thinking, remembering. "It seemed shorter than this."

"Shorter? You think something is wrong?" Marta Caine was genuinely afraid. They were in the Rift and in the Rift danger was always close. "Maurice! Earl! Carl—are you sure?"

"No, how can I be?" He bridled beneath her urgency. "It was years ago. But if you're worried I'll ask the steward."

"No," said Dumarest. "We'll ask the captain."

Frome matched his ship, a small, hard man with filed teeth over which his lips fitted like a trap. He scowled as he came to the door leading into the control room.

"You're off limits. Return to the salon at once."

"Willingly, Captain, as soon as you have eased our minds." Dumarest kept his voice casual. "We are a little concerned about the delay. Is something wrong with the ship?"

"No."

"I'm glad to hear it. The ladies were anxious. Then it's true we are being diverted? The steward mentioned—"

"What he shouldn't have done." Unthinkingly the captain fell into the trap. "The fool should have known better than to relay ship-business to passengers."

Dumarest said, flatly, "Our business too, Captain. Where are we heading?"

"Harge."

"Harge?" Carl Santis thrust himself forward, his face ugly. "I booked to Fendris. I can't afford the delay."

"You leave the ship on Harge. You all leave it."

Dumarest dropped his hand to the mercenary's arm, feeling the tense muscle as he restrained Santis's lunge. Frome was armed, a laser holstered at his waist, one hand resting close to the butt—an unusual addition to any captain's uniform and a sure sign that he anticipated trouble. The navigator too was armed. He stood back in the control room, his weapon aimed at the group beyond the door.

Kemmer snapped, "That isn't good enough. I demand an explanation."

"Demand?" Frome bared his pointed teeth. "Demand?"

The trader had courage. "A deal was made, passage booked, money handed over. A high passage to Fendris. That's what I paid for and that's what I want."

"What you paid for was passage to my next planet of call and that's exactly what you're getting."

"You—"

"It should have been Fendris," said Dumarest quickly. Kemmer was about to lose his temper and, once antagonized, the captain would tell them nothing. He might even use his laser—Frome was the type. "But in space things can happen," continued Dumarest evenly. "The unexpected and the dangerous and the more so when in the Rift. Is that what happened, Captain? Some danger you had to avoid?"

"A warp," said Frome after a moment. "We hit one and it created strain in the generator. To proceed to Fendris would be to take too big a risk. That's why I headed for Harge." He added, "We'd have landed by now if it hadn't been for the storm."

The girl was careless, setting down the cup with too great a force so that the delicate china rang and a little tisane slopped from the container to puddle in the saucer. A puddle she quickly removed with the hem of her dress but the damage had been done and the very act of cleaning the mess had been an affront. To use the hem of her dress! The action of a common strumpet in a low tavern or of a slut from the Burrows!

"My lady, will that be all?"

"Yes." Even the thick tones of the girl created irritation. "No! Take the cup away. The saucer too, you fool! And change into a clean dress."

And, she thought, for God's sake learn how to act like a product of civilization instead of an ignorant, stupid peasant. Words she left unsaid as the girl picked up the tisane and hurried it from the room. Alone Ellain Kiran stared at the window.

A swirling brown grayness stared back.

An illusion, of course, the dust didn't possess eyes but always when looking at the wind-blown grains she could see them; the eyes of the dead, the eyes of those who would die and were even now dying. And other eyes, less human, those of the inimical forces which created the storms, the dust, the death it carried. The hatred of nature for man and his works. The eyes of a thing bent on destruction.

And yet, still, it held a strange and tormented beauty.

It drew her closer, naked feet padding over the tufted carpet, her gown rustling as the fabric dragged over the surface of a low table, small chimes spilling from disturbed bells. A tintinnabulation she ignored as, halting, she stared at the smooth curve of the plastic, the fury of the storm beyond.

The air, the dust, all were joined in seething turmoil. Winds sweeping from the distant mountains, lifting sands from the deserts, catching them, driving them in a composite whole. Grains of silica, basalt, granite, manganese. Crystalline particles formed of minute rubies, agates, diamonds, emeralds. The detritus of ancient cataclysms which had taken the mineral wealth of Harge and pulverized it and spread it wide and far to be the sport of surging winds. Crystals each facet of which were knives, each point a needle. Carried by the winds at fantastic velocities, they scoured the world.

Nothing unprotected could live a moment in such a blast. Even the toughest suit and thickest pane would fret and wear and shred into particles. Cracks would form, widen, open to expose the skin and flesh and muscle beneath. A moment and it would be ripped away by the ravening fury of countless minute teeth. Even now men lost in the storm could be dying, screaming as the acid of the blast flayed them raw, turning them into grinning parodies of men before even bone and teeth vanished with the rest.

The thought created a tension in her loins and she shuddered, drawing a deep breath, inflating her chest as she stared at the fury beyond the window. The pane itself was unmarked, protected from the scouring dust by an electronic field which kept the particles at bay. An expensive installation but one Yunus could afford. As he could afford so much.

She looked down and saw her hand, the fingers spread, the skin pale in the soft light from the room. Yunus Ambalo, a member of the Cinque; the five families which owned Harge. The Ambalo, Yagnik, Khalil, Barrocca and Tinyeh owning water, food, power, accommodation and transportation. On Harge you lived by their sufferance or you didn't live at all.

The hand had closed into a fist, the nails digging into her palm and in imagination she could feel that same hand closed around her body, holding her, tightening, making her a helpless prisoner of the Cinque. How long could she retain even a fraction of personal integrity? How long before she turned into something as coarse and crude as the girl who had served her?

Outside the dust turned black, lights brightening within the room, the pane becoming a mirror holding her reflection. An image taken from a tapestry; tall, the oval face slashed with a generous mouth betraying in its sensuosity, the eyes, deep-set, vividly green. The hair which hung like a cascade of flame, ruby tints reflected from cheeks and chin and the long column of her throat. The body hugged by gossamer fabrics, the fullness of breasts and hips emphasized by the narrow waist.

"Beautiful! Ellain, my darling, you are beautiful!"

Another image joined her own in the reflective pane, this taken from a frieze; the face of stone, flared nostrils, a cleft chin, a dark mass of hair tightly curled on a peaked skull, the nose aquiline, arrogant, proud. A man taller than herself who stepped close to stand behind her, arms circling her body, the hands rising, cupped, toward her breasts.

Hands which closed to rest on her shoulder blades as she turned to look up into his smiling face, seeing the smile turn into a frown, the amber eyes blaze then turn cold as, deftly, she slipped from the circle of his embrace.

"No, Yunus."

"You object? But why? May not a man appreciate beauty?"

"From a distance, yes."

"This to me?" Again a controlled anger burned in the cat-like eyes. "Is the past so easily forgotten?"

"The past is just that—the past." She moved from the window as the cloud of ebon dust yielded to a swirl of paler hue; chalk white touched with scabrous gray laced with somber umber flecked with pearl. "You presume too much."

"Presume?" His gesture embraced the room, the soft furnishings, the things of value which graced the surfaces of small tables, pedestals, cabinets. Statuettes, carved gems, small figurines some in suggestively erotic poses, others screaming in silent agony. In a bowl stood crystalline flowers with petals exuding an induced scent; rich, heavy and sensuous odors which hung like fragrant clouds over the shimmering petals. "Must I remind you to whom this belongs?"

"You own the room," she admitted. "The whole, damned apartment and everything in it. But never make the mistake of thinking you own me."

A matter he could have argued but knew better than to press the point. Later, perhaps, when his interest had waned and she annoyed him too much with her stubborn independence, but not now. Now it pleased him to be gracious, acting the sophisticate, crossing the room with casual indifference to pour wine from a crystal decanter into goblets engraved with interwound figures of classical proportions.

"The storm," he said gently. "Always you are like this during a storm. And yet your very anger accentuates your loveliness. And I? I cannot help but to respond."

"You flatter me, Yunus."

"When has truth ever been flattery?" Smiling, he handed her one of the goblets. "Come, let us drink to a cessation of hostilities between us. To your beauty, my dear! May it never wane!"

A toast in which she could join—God help her should she ever grow ugly. The thought of it made her swallow the wine, feeling its warm comfort as it ran down her throat to blossom in her stomach. His smile grew wider as she handed him the empty container.

"More?"

"No." She touched her throat, long fingers caressing the larynx, the silken sheen of the skin. "If I am to perform I must stay in condition. I assume you want me to perform?"

"Of course. But—"

"Don't be tiresome, Yunus. Your generosity has bought my voice not the use of my body." She saw the sudden tension of muscle at the edge of his jaw, the tautening of the skin over the knuckles of the hand which held his goblet. Quickly she added, "I'm sorry. The wine, the storm—please forgive me!"

For a moment she thought that, this time, she had gone too far, and cursed herself for her stupidity. To have called such a man tiresome! The insult was enough for him to take a vicious revenge. To have her taken and stripped and staked out on the sand. To let the wind-driven dust flay her alive. To turn the beauty he professed to admire into a shrieking nightmare of bloody horror.

Why had she been such a fool?

"You will forgive me, Yunus?" Then, as he made no answer, she continued, "Where do you wish me to sing? Here? At a private assembly? In public?"

"Not in public." Slowly he set down the goblet. Straightening, he turned to face her and she noticed the hard cruelty of his mouth, the implacable anger in his eyes. "I had intended for you to entertain a few selected guests; those who have the sensitivity and understanding to appreciate your talent. Now I am not sure if it would be wise."

"Because of what I said?" She guessed the answer and knew, with sudden insight, that to crawl now would be a mistake. "I did not say you were tiresome, Yunus, I asked you not to be. A foolish remark, perhaps, but hardly the cause for such annoyance. From a child I would have expected such a tantrum but not from a grown man. And even less from a man of your sophistication." Her laughter was the chiming of bells. "Come, my dear, let us drink again."

"And risk your purity of tone?"

"For you, yes. Please?"

She relaxed as he poured the wine, enjoying her triumph, enjoying too, now that it was over, the battle and danger she had tasted, the risk she had run. A small risk, perhaps, even Yunus would hardly dare face the displeasure of the Cinque by taking such a personal revenge as she had imagined, but, if driven too far, he would defy the universe and do or have it done.

And, always, she had enjoyed playing with fire.

She smiled as she took the proffered goblet and turned as she sipped to face the window. The dust was thin now, gusting, forming plumes as the dying wind released its hold. Already the maintenance crews would be busy with scoops and blowers to clear the vents and ports. More would be using heavy-duty lasers to fuse the sides of dunes and form paths, to support threatening masses and hold the dust in the configurations it had adopted. Temporary measures—the next storm would negate all they could do.

"You will sing," he said as he joined her. "Three songs and I leave it to you to determine which they shall be." A command—his tone softened as she nodded. "And afterward we can enjoy other entertainment. Sabinnus has a new dancer."

"A rival?"

"No, my dear, you are beyond compare. In any case she lacks grace. He found her in the Burrows, so I understand, or at least that is what he says. It adds to her attraction." He added, casually, "She dances between blades of naked steel."

And those watching would be eager for her to cut feet and legs, more interested in the spectacle of blood rather than a display of art. Ellain lifted the goblet and drank the last of the wine. The sting of alcohol would lull her precision a little but only an expert would notice the loss of purity. Those she had been ordered to entertain would be more interested in her body than her voice. The scarlet gown, then? The color would accentuate that of her hair or, no, it would be better to complement it rather than provide a match. Green, then? Or the tunic of gold which gave full revealment to her legs? Or something simple yet enticing in dusty black?

"Ellain?"

"I was thinking, trying to decide what to wear at your party. It is a party?"

"More of an assembly. A few friends to discuss certain matters of mutual interest. You will provide a diversion."

The black then, the bodice arranged so as to display her bosom, the skirt adjusted to show her thigh through the slit—old tricks which twisted her lips in a reminiscent smile. How old Teen Veroka, her music teacher and singing master, would have raved at such a blatant display. But he was on another world, probably dead by now, and she had long since learned the value of such exhibitionism. But to dress well she needed a maid.

Yunus shrugged when she mentioned it. "You have a maid. A new girl."

"A clumsy fool. What does she know of how to dress hair? To arrange a gown? What happened to Julie?" She saw his face turn blank in the fading mirror of the window. "Never mind. You will find someone capable? I want to look my best for your friends."

"I shall attend to it."

"And after the assembly? You mentioned entertainment."

He smiled, knowing her needs, his voice a purr to match the amber of his eyes as, leaning close, he whispered in her ear.

"Anything you wish, my darling. Men stripped and sweating as they wrestle for a prize. Others pounding at each other with metal gloves? Women wagering their skill against a score of rodents." Pausing, he let the images build. "Blood and pain," he whispered. "The arena?"

"Yes," she gasped. "Yes!"

Her goblet fell to join his on the floor as his hands rose, cupped, rising to her breasts. And this time she did not turn from the embrace.

Chapter Two

The place was a windowless chamber, the walls, roof and floor of fused sand, minute flecks of silica glinting in the glare of overhead lighting. The tables were the same, the benches, even the plates and pots—fused sand, the cheapest building material on Harge. Leaning with his back against a wall Dumarest looked over the tavern. Aside from the material with which it was built it was the same as countless others he had seen. A room with tables at which to sit, a bar from which food and drinks were served, a low dais which could hold a small band of entertainers if any were available and willing to work for the thrown coins which would be their sole reward. Some serving girls, vapid faces, careless as to dress, willing to titivate for the sake of tips and even to do more if the gain was high enough.

The clientele was also in the pattern; men killing time, others whispering as they made plans, many who just sat and watched, some who tried to drown their desperation in wine, a few who came for reasons of curiosity, others who found entertainment in mixing with those of different station. But this held something most others lacked and which pervaded the atmosphere like a subtle but disquieting perfume.

"Fear," said Carl Santis. "The place stinks of it." He sat on a bench next to Kemmer and held his pot in one, scarred hand. His face above the stained and worn clothing was beaked, the nose like the thrusting bill of a bird of prey. Scar tissue gleamed in the light, small patches of glisten against the swarthy complexion. Patches matched by those on his tunic where the weight of protective armor had polished the nap. Sure signs of the mercenary's trade. "Fear," he said again. "It smells like a camp of raw recruits waiting to engage."

Waiting to fight, to gamble with life and death, but for

those in the room there was no waiting. The battle to survive never ceased and death could come as a blessing.

"Harge," said Kemmer. "They should have named it Hell." He lifted his pot and sipped then lowered it to scowl at the wine. "Frome, the bastard! Dumping us the way he did. One day, with luck, we'll meet again."

"Armed," mused Santis. "Did he wear a gun when you booked passage, Earl?"

If he had, Dumarest would have waited for another ship. He said, "No. Did any of you ask if he'd be willing to carry you on?"

"Marta did." Kemmer sipped again at his wine, his mouth looking as if he'd tasted acid. "She asked if he'd take her once he'd effected repairs. He wasn't interested."

"Odd." Santis frowned. "Easy money from an old woman who couldn't cause trouble. Why turn down a profit?"

"He dumped us," said the trader. "All of us. He'd been paid. That lie about repairs was obvious." He looked baffled. "But why? What was behind it? What do the people here hope to gain?"

The money they carried and the labor they could provide—the normal reason for isolated communities bribing captains to dump their passengers. Once landed and in debt they would be helpless to leave, forced to work as contract-labor to clear a steadily accumulating mountain of debt. Slaves in all but name and far more economical to keep.

"It doesn't make sense," said the trader. He had been brooding on the matter. "Mettalus has already fixed up an apartment for himself and the girl and can live in comfort until they can take a ship. Marta has a room—I offered to share but she would have none of it."

"A mistake," said Santis. "If she hopes to set up in business she's due for a shock. There's too much competition for anyone of her age to stand a chance."

"As I told her," agreed Kemmer. "She didn't take it too well. That leaves us. I'm too soft to do a hard day's work and Santis is too old to take willingly to a pick. And what use would they have for a mercenary? Which leaves you, Earl." He chuckled at the humor of what he next suggested. "Maybe we've all been dumped on your account. It could be someone wants you held somewhere until they can collect you. If so they've chosen a damned good place."

And it was a damned good guess if guess it was. From

where he sat Dumarest studied the trader, looking at the eyes, the hands, the movements of the small muscles around the mouth. An agent? It was possible; the Cyclan employed all types, but he doubted it. The man was too much in character to be playing a part. And there would be no reason for the dumping if he had not been what he seemed. Santis the same, Marta Caine also and the other two could be eliminated; the girl was too young to have learned effective deception and Grish Metallus had been aboard the *Urusha* long before Dumarest had asked for passage. No proof, but even the Cyclan had limitations governed by time and distance, and not everyone could be an agent. Yet Dumarest had no doubt as to why they had been dumped.

Kemmer was right—someone wanted him held.

And Harge was a prison.

He rose and walked over to the bar, ignoring the glares of women who felt robbed of a tip, ordering another pot of wine and looking around as it was poured. Had Frome been contacted direct? In the Rift radio-communication was unreliable at the best of times what with the electronic furnaces of suns set close filling the ether with static and electro-magnetic distortion. Had he been paid to dump any passengers he might have been carrying? Had other captains?

"Here!" The bartender slammed down the pot. "That's sixteen kren." He scooped up the coins. "Just landed?"

"Yes."

"Welcome to Harge. On business?"

"Call it an unavoidable visit. Any other ships arrived recently?"

"One since the storm. That must be yours. Two just before—fifteen and seventeen days ago. None before that for three weeks. Then we had a ten-day storm—or was it twelve?"

"You get many storms?"

"It's the season." He met Dumarest's eyes. "Quite a few. I guess you're interested in ships, eh? They land when they can and leave without delay. Yours has gone. The *Urusha*, right? Took off as soon as the cargo was loaded."

"We had to wait to land. Is that normal?"

"If a storm is blowing itself out. Sometimes they move on and forget us unless it's a charter or special delivery. It depends. From space they can get a clear view of the situation and act accordingly. Travel much?"

"No."

"I thought not." The man accepted the lie. "You talk pretty green. Got any money?"

"Some."

"Watch it. That advice I'll give you for free. I'll mind it for you if you want."

"Thanks, but I'll manage."

"Yes," said the man. "Yes, I guess you can."

He turned to serve a girl with a torn skirt and cheap bracelets adorning pimpled arms who was waiting on a group at one of the tables. Dumarest halted beside them, chatted, moved on to stand beside a pair studying a chart, left them to talk to a waitress to whom he gave money.

As he rejoined the others Santis said, "Learn anything?"

"Nothing of use."

"What is there to learn?" Kemmer brooded over his wine. "The need to survive? We know that. The need to cooperate? We know that too but how seldom it is done. And can one man be expected to aid another when that aid robs him of life?" He added, "Thieves here receive drastic punishment."

Santis was curt, "So?"

"I mention it, nothing more."

"Do I look like a man who would steal? Fight, yes, kill too if the pay is right, but steal?"

"If it meant your life, yes," said Dumarest. "I think you would. I could be wrong but, if so, we are both fools." He waited a moment then, as the mercenary made no comment, said, "One small item which may be of interest. At times men are employed to work on outside installations."

"Debtors," said Kemmer. "They have a list. I could have saved you the bribe you gave to the waitress."

"A few coins," protested Santis. "Less than the price of a drink."

"But money!" Kemmer lowered his voice. "You mercenaries are all the same—easy come easy go. Your pay is something to get rid of before you get killed. The only ones who really gain from a war are the merchants and vendors of delights. But a trader knows the value of a coin. It can spell the difference between profit and loss. Tell me, honestly now, how wealthy are you?"

"I had enough for passage to Fendris. There I could have found employment but the chance is lost now."

"And?"

Santis said, bleakly, "I lack the cost of a high passage."

"I am better than you," said Kemmer. "Not much but enough for me to insist I buy the next round. Even so unless a vessel comes soon I shall be in dire trouble. The fee to gain entry—" He drew out his cheeks. "Earl?"

"We're all in the same situation. Marta?"

"Has money but I don't know how much. But it will do us no good. She will neither lend nor give and, frankly, I don't blame her." Kemmer shook his head. "Life, at times, can be hard."

And on Harge more than hard. Dumarest leaned back, his shoulders hard against the wall, an instinctive position which gave maximum protection. A caution which was now too late. His questions had gained more than he'd divulged. The passengers on earlier ships had not been dumped—Frome had been the first captain to have done so. Which meant he must have had a special reason and Dumarest was certain now what it was.

The Cyclan, plotting, predicting where and when he would be, calculating his movements on the basis of assembled data, extrapolating the most logical sequence of events. The Rift had originally spelled safety but the very plethora of worlds, short journeys and plentiful small ships had finally told against him. Now, it seemed, his luck had run out. Harge was a prison. One bounded by wind and dust, lacerating storms and economic factors no less cruel.

The entry fee had been high and gave nothing but the right to shelter. Each sip of water and scrap of food would have to be paid for. Each moment of rest. Even his present comfort was limited by the amount of drinks purchased and already a woman was approaching to take their order or demand they leave. There were no heavy industries, no open fields, no chance of finding work and building a stake. Soon, like Santis, he would be without the cost of a passage. Every traveler's nightmare—to be stranded on a world from which he couldn't escape. To die there—but Dumarest had no fear of that. The Cyclan would come to claim him first.

The assembly was as she'd expected; the rich and powerful exhibiting their possessions. Jashir Yagnik had a juggler, a clown who filled the air with spinning orbs and turned and danced and grimaced with pretended terror which grew real when, fumbling a ball, he saw the expression on his patron's

face. Khan Barrocca had a clairvoyant, an albino who tittered and clutched her breasts and foamed from bloodless
lips as she spouted frenzied gibberish. Even fat old Keith
Ambalo, Yunus's uncle, was disgusted and made no attempt
to disguise it.

"For God's sake, Khan, get rid of that thing. She's enough
to turn my stomach."

"I thought you'd be amused."

"I'm not." Old and powerful Keith Ambalo could afford to
indulge in the luxury of discourtesy. "Standards should be
maintained. Yunus, my boy, where's that singer of yours?"

She was seated beside him, tall resplendent in an ebon
gown, her hair shimmering with an inner effulgence, the blaze
of scarlet giving a translucent luster to her skin. It was a
measure of his contempt for all beings not of the Cinque that
he chose to ignore her. It was a measure of her pride that she
risked being discourteous in turn.

"Yunus, you didn't tell me! How sad that your uncles eyes
are failing!"

"Failing?" He frowned then, catching the meaning, hesitated between rage and laughter. To mock his family was un-
forgivable and yet Keith did make himself ridiculous at
times. And it would do no harm to take Ellain's side—Khan,
at least, would be pleased. "A recent development," he said
seriously. "He cannot see anything which does not belong to
him. Nor anything he envies and cannot obtain. But there is
nothing wrong with his ears."

"Ears? What are you thinking about? What—" He stut-
tered to a brief silence then, with a shrug, continued, "Have
your joke, my boy. Laugh at an old man while you can. But
at least let me hear something worth listening to while I am
your guest." His eyes swiveled toward Ellain. "If you would
accommodate me, my dear, I would be grateful."

"Yunus?"

He delayed his permission, selecting a sweetmeat from a
selection on a salver of precious metal, biting into it with a
flash of strong, white teeth. A childish display of arrogance
but one which had to be tolerated. Only when he had finished
the morsel did he nod.

"Go ahead, my dear. It is time we had some entertainment
worthy of our station."

The musicians were assembled at the end of the chamber;
a small group but equipped with electronic devices which ex-

tended their range. She conferred with them for a moment, emphasized certain points and then took her position. A moment then, as the lights began to dim and the soft sounds of controlled vibrations welled from the musicians behind her, she began to sing.

She had chosen to begin with Remsley's *Banachata*, a relatively simple piece but one holding unsuspected difficulties for the novice with its abrupt changes of key and tempo. Teen Veroka had used it as a test piece and had been scathing in his comments to those who failed to perform to his satisfaction. She had not failed and it was a good choice to set the mood for the songs to follow: Hezekiah's *Passion of the Heart* and Ecuilton's *Interlude*. But now she needed to concentrate on the *Banachata*.

It began softly, slowly, suddenly rising to a shrill and almost raucous scream, to fall undulatingly over octaves to throb like a drum then to blur into a formless stream of incoherent words which stimulated the imagination of those who listened, guiding them to fit their own patterns, their own concepts. Tonal magic enhanced by the sounding board of chest and throat, projected, modulated by larynx and tongue, lips and teeth, rising from the stomach as muscles, and training turned her entire body into a living facsimile of the pipe of an organ, a flute, the wail of a fife, the sonorous echo of a drum.

She held them, after the first few moments she knew it. The gown, the display of flesh, all were unnecessary, her vocal magic was enough. Khan Barrocca sat, a goblet half-raised to his lips, his desire for wine forgotten in his appreciation of her art. Jashir Yagnik brooded, his face betraying his envy, his eyes his need. Chole Khalil, young, impressionable, stared at her body but saw only the imagery of his dreams. Yunus, Keith, the others assembled with their toys—all were in the hollow of her hand. An audience to manipulate, to control. And, suddenly, she was a child again sitting in the great auditorium of the Opera House, looking, listening, knowing with every cell of her body what her destiny must be. To sing. To create rapture. To deliver joy.

The *Banachata* drew toward its end, shrill, clear notes wafting like birds, caught, amplified, engaged in a mesh of grace-notes, the main theme rising to fall to rise again in a calculated sonic wave which matched the aural emotional triggers inherent in all who were human. Science wedded to art and served as entertainment.

The piece ended with a sharp abruptness, the silence shocking, stunning, then, before the spell could be broken, she began the second selection.

Hezekiah had worked on it for half his life and had died still unsatisfied but few would admit that he had achieved less than perfection. This time there were words all could follow, each syllable chosen for semantic and emotive impact, the music accentuating the message as her own skill modulated it, tone and key changing, pure melody providing contrast, long ululations stretching and distorting time. A tapestry of sound and music, words and tone, cadences weaving as threads, glissades, apparent cacophonies, the final, triumphant cadenza.

This time she waited for applause, bowing, smiling as Barrocca hurled down his goblet in order to beat his hands, Yagnik rising to cry out, a sound born of emotion, torn from his soul. Chole Khalil joined him, adding to the storm rising from the table. Even Yunus clapped and his uncle dented a salver with the impact of a spoon.

Slowly the room regained its calm. Silence came to replace the din but only when it was complete did she give the signal to the watchful musicians. With a chord as solemn as a prayer the *Interlude* began.

Ecuilton had been a child during the war which had ruined his planet. He had seen his mother die in a burning house, his father torn by explosives, his brother crisped by searing pastes. He had witnessed all the horror and vileness of internecine combat and, later, the indifference of the victors to what had happened to the vanquished. To them, as to the others, the thing had been a mere interlude. To him it was a thing he could never forget and, old, crippled and dying, he had created a masterpiece.

Ellain hated it.

She hated what it did to her, the emotions it aroused; the pain and fury and frustration. The injustice. The horror. The imagery of burning, screaming children, of shrieking, distraught women. Of men crawling like half-crushed insects, blind, groping, entrails trailing like greasy ribbons. Of boots stamping on pleading, extended hands. Of the bewildered cries of helpless babies starving as they sucked at the breasts of raped and murdered mothers. The violation of the soil. The stink, the filth, the obscenity of war.

Hated it and yet loved it too. Enjoyed it in part and echoed that enjoyment to match the bleak despair. Feeling the tension mount in her loins, the hardening of her nipples as she sang of blood and pain; a sexual stimulus matched by the disgust of those who warred against the helpless. A contradiction of civilized mind and primitive nature which created, for her, a vibrant excitement. Often she ended the *Interlude* shuddering in orgasm.

But not this time. Now she controlled her emotions, resisting the impulse to yield to the spell of the tonal and musical magic, projecting, aiming the notes like bullets at her audience. As the last rose to hang quivering like a scream, to end with the impact of a fist, she bowed, hair cascading to mound on the floor, one long thigh exposed to gleam in the subdued light, the lines of her back illuminated by the spotlight which had shone throughout her performance.

And again the room quivered to the thunder of applause.

"My dear!" Yunus rose to greet her as she neared the table. "You were wonderful! Superb!"

He was gratified, basking in the adulation given by the others to his toy. A matter of pride, equal to that felt by the owner of a winning horse, the possessor of an intelligent dog. And yet, as he touched her, she felt that there could be something more. A tenderness. A regard. Surely she must mean more to him than a voice to beguile his guests?

Then Khan Barrocca said, "Yunus, I offer ten thousand kren for her contract."

"Only ten?" Yunus shrugged. "You aim too low, my friend."

"A hundred!" Young Chole gulped, recognizing his temerity. "A hundred thousand, Yunus!"

She waited for him to reject the offer, to make it plain to all that he regarded her as beyond price. Instead he said, musingly, "You tempt me, Chole. A hundred, you say?"

"Yes."

"And you have it?" He smiled at the other's hesitation. "No? Well, approach me again when you do."

The smile had betrayed his nature, it had held more cruelty than amusement and it had not been kind to have made sport of the boy. Yet the offer, if nothing else, had restored some of her lost confidence. Why need she be so dependent on Yunus Ambalo? She was unique while he was but one of many—a fact she had tended to forget.

"No, my dear," he said quietly, and it was as if he'd read her mind. "I am not to be discarded so easily. You must remember that it is I who own your contract. It is to me you are indebted."

She said, bitterly, "Could I ever forget it?"

"It would be wise if you did not."

"And you will see to it that I am reminded I am your property. Your slave!" Anger turned her eyes into emerald pools. "One day, Yunus! One day—"

"One day the winds will cease and the surface of Harge be as pleasant to walk on as—Nyadoma? That is the name of your world, isn't it? Nyadoma where all are equal and none are denied." His tone was dry with mocking. "I wonder why you ever left such a paradise." Then, with sudden acidity, he added, "Never threaten me, Ellain. Not when we are alone or in company. Forget and you will regret it. That I promise."

"As you promised to take me to the arena?"

"Of course, my dear. I hadn't forgotten." His smile was bland. "But first let us finish the meal."

Harge was a box holding a world and though small it held all the elements of a planet. The upper towers held expensive suites and apartments, windowed, the panes protected from the dust, the air itself balanced to a scented delight. There it was possible to wander in exotic gardens, swim in limpid pools, lounge beneath transparent roofs in the light of sun or stars. Lower were more modest apartments, offices, walks and shops, schools. Lower still, below ground level, began a different world, one of noise and smells and harsh bleakness. And lower still, as deep as it was possible to get, the Burrows, the area of the damned.

Between the upper and lower worlds, like a thin film of oil, of insulation, was the place Dumarest knew had to exist.

"Come here, my pretty!" An old crone yelled a raucous invitation as he neared her stall. "Sit and let me study your palm. The future lies in the lines, your past, dangers which could threaten. Advantages too which could be lost unless anticipated." A leer disfigured her seamed features. "A girl lusting for just such a man as you and willing to pay for her pleasure. I can tell you where such are to be found. Rich women from the upper levels and generous if satisfied. Come, sit, cross my palm with silver and let's begin."

Kemmer grunted. "Why waste money? The woman is a fraud."

Her eyes were sharp. "A fraud, am I? Trader, who has cheated the most? Dare you let me tell your friends how you came to leave home?"

"Guesswork." Santis shrugged. "I could do as well."

"Which is why you are so rich, mercenary. So well supplied with food and wine and willing women. So respected. So much in demand." Her laughter rose, thin, brittle. The odors of rancid grease and pungent spices strengthened as she lifted an arm and pointed at Dumarest. "You, my pretty, come and sit with me. Last night I had a dream and you fit the vision. A man dressed in gray with a look on his face which woke me screaming. A dire omen and you would be a fool to ignore it."

And perhaps a bigger fool to yield to her blandishments, but Dumarest, wise in the ways of carnival, sensed more than the others. The crone was trying too hard and how had she known Kemmer was a trader? The mercenary was obvious but the other could only have been a shrewd guess. And, if nothing else, she could tell him things useful to know.

The booth was small, decorated with gaudy symbols, the devices painted on the ubiquitous fused sand. A table bore a crystal ball, the surface scratched and dull. The cloth beneath was stained, frayed and torn in a few places. The chairs were of thin metal designed to be folded for portability. Incense fumed from a metal pot and hung in an odorous cloud beneath the ceiling.

As he sat the old woman held her hand before him, palm uppermost. Silently she watched as he dropped coins into the grimed cup.

Quietly he said, "I'm no gull, mother. Don't waste your time feeding me a line of rich wantons or hidden treasure. I've grafted in my time and know the angles. Just answer a few questions and be honest. A deal?"

Her hand closed over the coins. "Don't be too clever, my friend. And don't be too mistrustful. I have the power. Give me your hand." She took it, spreading the fingers and crouched brooding over the palm. A stained nail traced lines, halted at juxtapositions, hesitated at certain points. "A traveler," she murmured. "One who has seen many worlds. One too who has had many loves. One who has known much danger. A fighter trained in the use of a blade. A gambler. A

searcher after truth who—" She broke off, inhaling sharply.
"Red," she whispered. "Scarlet—beware the color of blood!"

Dumarest watched, restraining his impatience. His clothing
alone would have told her he was a traveler; garb designed
for wear and protection. The knife in his boot coupled with
the callouses on his palm would have told he used a blade
and all men who fought were, in essence, gamblers.

"Scarlet," she said again. "It is behind you, around you, all
is scarlet."

Another guess? Dumarest said, "Are there any here who
wear scarlet robes?" The shake of her head meant little; cybers could reside in the upper levels and she need never know
it. "Has anyone asked after me? By description, naturally."

"No."

"Would you know?"

"If they asked in the Stril I would know. I get to hear most
things." Again she studied his palm. "There's something odd
here. A danger but more than that. You've killed," she accused. "There are men who have cause to hate you. Vengeful
men."

"So?"

"They will give you no rest. And they are close, close. I
see—no, some things are best not told."

"We had a deal," said Dumarest, flatly. "If that's the best
you can do then I'm going to feel cheated. You wouldn't
want me to feel that, would you? No, I thought not. Now
why not just answer a few questions?"

The others joined him as he left the booth. Kemmer made
no secret of hiding his irritation at what he considered rank
stupidity; Santis was more sympathetic.

"Sometimes it helps, Earl, I know that. Once on Pico I visited a palmist. We were set to attack at dawn and I was trou-
bled. Something sent me to her and her warnings caused me
to change the plans. I attacked from a different direction
three hours early and found they were set and ready for me.
If I'd followed the original plan we'd have been blasted to
atoms. As it was we won."

"So what did you learn, Earl?" Kemmer scowled at a painted harlot who caught at his arm. As she fell back with a
screamed insult he added, "A way out of this mess?"

There was only one way out and they knew it and in the
Stril it could be found. Dumarest led the way through passages lined with booths, past vendors of assorted and exotic

delights, ignoring the touts, pimps and harlots. Once he halted to drive the heel of his palm against the chin of a man who lingered too close too long, sending the pickpocket staggering back with empty hands and vacant eyes. At a junction he heard a familiar drone.

"Back the winner and pick up twice what you put down. The red fights the yellow. Roll up! Roll up! The next bout is about to commence!"

The spieler was tall, gaunt, his clothing shabby, his eyes restless. Behind him a chamber held a circular barrier centered with a table on which stood a dome of clear plastic. Now it was empty but for a thin, blue vapor but, once activated, clouds of red and yellow spores would be released to fight, to fall, the victors feeding on the vanquished to display the winning hue.

"Red and yellow, back your choice. Hurry! Hurry! Hurry! The next bout is about to commence!"

His words faded, were replaced by others yelled from a stunted, leather-lunged man who strutted on bowed legs.

"Three temple dancers from Fecundis—need I say more? Witness the immaculate purity of their movements. See with your own eyes the hidden mysteries of a secret cult. Watch as they perform exotic movements of tantalizing delight and, for a small fee, participate. You, sir!" His finger stabbed at Santis. "Age rests on your shoulders—before the doors of life close why not indulge in an experience you will never forget? Fifty kren to watch—another hundred to mount the platform. A bargain!" His voice rose as they moved on. "You refuse the offer? What has happened to the men of Harge?"

A simpering woman could have told him as she displayed the charms of veiled and lissom girls. An apothecary, eyes blank, droned the offer of charms and love philtres, medicines and salves for annoying ailments. A magician ate fire and produced eggs from unlikely places. A boxer, knotted with rope-like muscle, offered to take on all comers.

"You there!" His manager, eager for trade, thrust his hand toward Dumarest. "A hundred kren if you last a minute. Five hundred if you leave the ring the winner. Your friends can see fair play."

"Five hundred," said Kemmer. "For a smashed face and broken bones."

For bruises and internal injuries; a ruptured liver or spleen, broken ribs thrusting jagged ends into lungs and membranes.

The boxer had fists like hammers and would use them as such. Dumarest studied the face and eyes, seeing and recognizing the dullness, the lack of interest. A man who had fought too hard and too often. A living machine lacking sense and feeling. One day the ruined cells in his brain would send him toppling in paralysis or death; until then he was fit for nothing but to kill.

Santis said, "Why isn't he fighting in the arena?"

"He is too gentle," said the manager quickly. "Too reluctant to hurt. A kindly creature who wants only to demonstrate his skill. Win and you will be paid. Lose and you can tell all your friends that you have faced and fought with a champion."

"For a hundred kren, you say?" A burly youth with a painted girl hanging on his arm, eager to display his masculinity and win her favors, thrust himself toward the booth. "A hundred?"

"Last for a single minute and it's yours. Five times as much if you win. Step forward now! Hurry! Hurry!"

Dumarest moved on as the youth, pressed by a crowd eager to see blood and pain, entered the booth followed by those willing to pay to watch the combat. He could win if the boxer retained the ability to soften his blows and the manager had the sense to prime the crowd. An easy victory to encourage others to fight and their companions to bet. If so the youth would be lucky—but Dumarest wouldn't bet on it.

Santis said, "Ten years ago I might have taken him on. I was always good at unarmed combat."

"For five hundred? It isn't enough." Kemmer stepped to one side to allow a tall man with a strained and painted face a direct passage. The man had eyes like blank windows, the pupils enormous, a rim of white showing around the contracted iris. Froth edged his writhing lips and his hands, like claws, snapped at the air before him. Drugged, in delusion such a man could be dangerous. Uneasily he said, "Earl, are we close?"

The man had come from a narrow passage lit by a somber orange glow. Doors gaped like hungry mouths each adorned by symbols and suggestive illustrations, several filled with swirling mist shot with streaks and shafts of vivid color. The vending place of drugs and bizarre experiences, of mechanically induced stimulation and hypnotic dreams. Soft moans came from some of the doors, screams and frenzied cursing from others. In the dull illumination the figures of touts loomed like distorted ghosts.

"Full sensatapes," whispered one. "Burn, be hanged, be flayed, be boiled in oil—all genuine experiences recorded from the victims of actual executions. Be crucified, be impaled. . . ."

"Be the willing victim of a woman's lust," suggested another. "Writhe beneath the impact of demanding flesh your vigor constantly renewed. Be. . . ."

"A tiger, a spider, a hunting wasp." The offers were a susuration. "Taste blood and feel the crunch of bone and chiton. Learn. . . ."

"How to expand the senses. To feel the winds of space on your naked flesh. To imagine and see your imaginings take shape. To . . ."

"Be a God. With these new applications of science and medicine none need be denied the complete fullfillment of elementary desire. Adventure, enhance your psyche, know the joys of. . . ."

"Rest." The voice was a purr. "Lie and smoke and dream and forget the strife of survival. Find happiness and joy in pleasant vapors. A hundred kren buys you a couch for an hour."

A place in a mist of smoke where somnolent shapes lay in temporary oblivion. Figures which twitched at times and stirred and cried out as they rose from the euphoria of dreams or plunged deeper into the horror of nightmare. The last of the doorways. Beyond lay what Dumarest had come to find.

Chapter Three

Like the city the Stril was layered; parts catering to innocuous amusements, others dealing with those of stronger meat, a section close to Hell itself. Beyond the passage the roof soared over widened passages, a cleared space in which fountains cast a melodious tinkling, artificial breezes stirring artificial fronds. Statues stood staring with blind eyes, figures of men and women fashioned from the glazed and colored sand, the fused material, depicting scenes of torment and lust, of gaiety and wild abandon. A man, head thrown back, mouth open, hands clutching his ripped abdomen, screamed in an endless, silent agony. Two women locked in a compulsive embrace stared unseeingly at another impaled on a cone of milky crystal who screamed wordlessly at a crucified man who stared bleakly at a couple writhing in frozen ecstasy.

Statues by the hundred set in groups and lined array in the area which circumnavigated the central bulk of the area.

Dumarest looked at it, seeing the high, colonnaded wall, the arched gates and porticoes, the paths leading to the entrances. Worn stone and polished benches all showing the passage of use and time.

"What now, Earl?" Santis scowled as he looked around. The mercenary was no stranger to the forms of diversion always to be found in any civilized area but had never found them to his taste. To fight according to the rules and customs of war was one thing, to demean the brain and courage of a man was another. And no mercenary could have avoided seeing the degradation of which humans were capable. "This place stinks!"

Of sweat and fear and blood and exudations of pain and lust. Of greed and riches and abject poverty. Of desperation. To Dumarest they were familiar smells.

He said, "Among other things the crone told me they played Find the Jester here. She didn't lie."

Kemmer was impatient. "Well?"

"It gives us a chance to build up a stake. Carl, you handle the bets. Maurice, you back his play. I'll act as a block." Dumarest stared around, noticing small groups clustered between the statues, seeing one newly forming. "There! Let's move in fast!"

A man stood behind a narrow board, three cards in his hands, his voice a drone. "Find the jester and pick up double what you put down. Three cards, you see? A deuce, another deuce and a jester. I throw them down—so. Make your bets!"

His moves had been clumsy, the position of the jester obvious to all. A man standing at the end of the board, obviously drunk, slammed down a handful of coins and turned, coughing. Calmly the dealer moved the selected card, the jester, and exchanged it for one of the deuces. No one made a comment—who was to protect a fool from his own folly?

Dumarest knew better. The drunk was no fool but a man working with the dealer, acting the drunk to set up the crowd. There would be others and he spotted them, a plump man who would later lead the betting and another who stood ready to take care of any trouble. Dumarest edged toward him as the mercenary took his chance.

"A hundred!"

"Your money—"

"On the card!" Santis lifted his hand to reveal the coin resting on the pasteboard. A certain bet which others could have made but had allowed suspicion and natural reluctance to hold them back. The only certain bet they could have made. "I win?"

"You win." The dealer was phlegmatic. Sometimes a smart bastard moved in but it could help prime the other punters for the kill. He frowned as Santis repeated the maneuver. "Another hundred?"

"Five." The mercenary met his eyes. "I win again, yes?"

"He wins!" Kemmer yelled from where he stood in the crowd. "His money was down. I saw it—we all saw it. Pay him."

"That's right." The plump man made the best of a bad job. "His cash was down, I saw it." He turned his head and Dumarest saw the signal he gave with a flick of the eyes. "Good for you, Pop. You're on a winning streak."

One he was going to make certain would end. Like the actors they were they swung into a well-rehearsed charade. The dealer, taken with a sudden attack of coughing, dropped the cards and turned, doubled, fighting for breath. Quickly the plump man lifted the jester, displayed it and deliberately creased a corner. When the dealer recovered, the cards were as he had left them. Picking them up, he shuffled them, resuming his spiel.

"Find the jester and pick up double what you put down. No money no winnings. Have your cash ready. Here we go!"

The switch had been neatly done. Knowing what to look for, Dumarest failed to see it. The cards fell, the one with the creased corner obviously the jester. Hands heavy with coins thrust forward to take advantage of the plump man's obvious cheating. None felt sorry for the dealer—hadn't he robbed the drunk?

Calmly he turned the card, revealed a deuce and swept up the money.

As Santis edged from the board a man bumped into him.

"Watch it, old timer! That was my foot you trod on!"

"An accident—"

"Like hell it was!" The man stayed close, his hands busy. He sucked in his breath as Dumarest caught at one of his wrists. "What—"

"Bad luck," said Dumarest softly. "And all yours. You were outsmarted. We're going now. Try to stop us and I'll break your arm. You want that?" His voice was low but hard. As hard as his face, the grip of his fingers. "It's the luck of the game."

"You bastards! Did Syclax—"

"You'll be hearing from him." Dumarest released the man's wrist. "Get back to your game."

"Syclax?" Kemmer frowned as they moved away. "Do you know him?"

"No."

"But—"

"He must be a rival operator. A pitch is easy to ruin and punters easily scared. He could be trying to move in or be demanding protection. Forget it. We have other things to worry about."

Twice more Santis hit the card game and then Dumarest took a hand, betting on the whereabouts of a pea, resting a finger on his selected shell and smiling as he turned over the others to reveal their emptiness. Reluctantly the operator paid. As they left he called a man, whispered, sent him running down a path between the statues.

"That's it," said Santis. "Right, Earl?"

"That's what?" Kemmer frowned.

"The end of easy pickings." Dumarest glanced at the crowds, the little clusters. "We've been marked and will be spotted. Try to pull the same stunt again and we'll be blocked. Someone will accuse us of picking a pocket or cheating in some way. A drunk will pick a fight. Bets will be disallowed." He shrugged at the trader's expression. "You must have done the same thing yourself."

"At an auction, maybe. A ring—" Kemmer scowled. "There's a difference."

"No difference. Cheating is normal when a man needs to survive."

"There are ethics," protested Kemmer. "A trader can't afford to cheat if he hopes to stay in business. He may shade the truth a little but that's expected. It's up to the buyer to—" He broke off, blanching. "What the hell's that?"

A scream burst from a point at the end of the arena and brought a sudden stillness. It rose, echoing from the roof, a shriek of pure agony, torn, Dumarest guessed, from a dying throat. For a moment the stillness held; then, with a babbling susuration, the crowd resumed its business, only a handful running toward the source of the scream.

"The pits." A man gasped the information as Dumarest caught his arm and snapped a question. "Someone was unlucky."

A woman, still recognizable as such. A once-living creature now lying like a limp rag doll in a pool of her own blood. She was naked aside from a twist of fabric around breasts and loins, her legs scarred with bites, more on her stomach, back and arms. Old wounds blended with some healing, others freshly made. Other bodies, smaller, toothed and furred lay scattered around her in the pit.

Dumarest stood on the edge looking down. The place was circular, eight feet deep, the walls smooth, stained and flecked with ugly smears. From the edge the floor sloped sharply upward so as to allow the ring of those watching a clear view. A low parapet provided a measure of safety.

A pit—on other worlds they held bears, bulls, dogs, all

baited by other creatures smaller but more plentiful. On Harge they baited women.

A man stood in the pit with the body. He looked up, scowling, snapping orders as a pair of assistants made an appearance.

"Hurry, damn you! Time's money. Get this mess cleared up. Never mind washing down the walls; that can wait. Get some fresh sand for the floor." As they jumped to obey he sprang, caught the edge of the pit and hauled himself upright. To Dumarest he said, "Did you see it?"

"No."

"Heard it, then? What a scream. I didn't think she'd let go like that. The damned fool!" His face glowered and one hand clenched into a fist. "I warned her she was attempting too much but she wouldn't listen. Drugged, I guess, floating, riding high. Greedy to beat the clock. Well, they never learn."

"The clock?"

"Sure." The man glanced at Kemmer. "The prize is a thousand and they lose ten for every second. A score of rats is set against them—a skilled fighter can clear them in just over a minute. They use scents and oils to attract the beasts and catch them as they spring. If they put up a good show they get extra from the crowd. Bets are made on how long they take." He waved a hand at the dead woman now bundled in a sling. "She used to be good. Well, there'll always be others."

Flesh and blood driven by greed and pride to make a target for rodents. A human creature driven by hunger and desperation to fight and kill, to race the clock, to suffer the sting and burn of bites. To listen to the jeers of watching men, the shouts, the fall of coins tossed as largesse to a beggar.

And yet was he so different?

Dumarest stood, looking down, seeing another ring, a wider expanse. The arena in which he had fought so often, armed with naked steel, facing another equally armed, both intent on murder.

To listen to the roar of the crowd, to smell the fear and sweat and oil, to taste the stink of blood, to know the burn of wounds. A man or a rat—what was the difference? A fighter intent on killing or rodents fighting in blind panic to survive? To enter the ring from choice for the sake of reward or to be driven in with flame and goads?

Was he any better than a beast?

"Earl?" Kemmer was staring at him, his face creased, anxious. "Earl, is something wrong?"

The world, the way of civilization, the universe. Would men ever live as brothers? Some hoped they might but on Harge the monks of the Church of Universal Brotherhood were not allowed. The charity they extended was despised by the Cinque, the creed they preached regarded with suspicion and fear. The belief that all men were brothers and the pain of one was the pain of all. That if all could but look and accept the basic truth and recognize that *there, but for the grace of God, go I*, the millennium would have arrived.

And there, in the pit, but for the grace of God, he could be lying!

"The poor bitch," rumbled Santis. "There are better things for a woman to do." He watched as the bundle was carted away, blood still dripping from the ravaged throat. "The clock," he said bitterly. "If she earned a few hundred kren she'd be lucky. And for that she had to risk her life."

Again and again until, inevitably, the gamble would be lost. And yet what else could she have done?

What else could he do?

Dumarest said, "Let's get on with it. Maurice, you handle the money and place the bets. Get the best odds you can. Carl, you'll be my manager. Remember, I'm dull, stupid, slow and a nuisance. You want to be rid of me."

"Will they be interested?"

"Why not? Cheap prey and an easy win. Ask for Matpius." A name won from the crone. "He lacks any compunction. Maurice, take the money."

All of it—but Dumarest was gambling more than cash. If he lost, the others would be ruined but he would be dead.

And Matpius was willing to see him die.

He was a smooth, round, scented man with delicate hands heavily adorned with rings. His hair was dressed in elaborate ringlets which fell over his ears and clustered at the nape of his neck. His clothing matched the image, the tunic pleated, the sleeves slashed to reveal inner streaks of vivid hue. A wide belt supported the jewelled hilt of a dagger. He carried a pomander which he lifted to his nostrils before he spoke.

"A fighter? *That*?"

"A creature of misfortune, my lord." Santis, accustomed to dealing with the rich and influential, bowed. "A trained man of my old company who served me well and to whom I am obligated. And yet, you understand, an obligation can prove onerous. His mind is not as it was and he tends to become too great a liability. My honor, of course, will not let me see him starve and yet—" He broke off, shrugging. "We are both men of experience, my lord. I am sure you appreciate the situation."

Matpius sniffed at his pomander, eyes shrewd as he studied Dumarest who stood, eyes blank, shoulders stooped, hands dangling loosely at his sides. A fine, well-made man, tall and with a face the women would find appealing. A pity he lacked intelligence or, no, just as well he did not. Using him would create no problems.

"He carries a knife—why?"

"Habit, my lord. As a soldier he grew used to the weight of arms. I let him keep it." Santis leaned forward and drew the knife from Dumarest's boot, displaying the artfully dulled blade, the stained and apparently blunt edge. "You can accommodate me?"

"Perhaps." It was in the man's nature to keep others in suspense. Again Matpius sniffed at his pomander, calculating, thinking. Against a man this creature would stand little chance and those who came to the arena expected more than mere butchery. And yet drugs could stimulate him and drive him to a killing frenzy. In such a case the results might be interesting. "You are concerned as to his welfare?"

"My lord, I am a realist. Use him as you will. The fee—"

"A thousand kren." Matpius waved the pomander. "Take it or leave it."

"It is little, my lord."

"But can be increased with an intelligent wager. Need I say more?" Matpius let the silence grow, one which spoke its own language. "Take him to the pens. Ask for Delman. Here." He scribbled a note. "Give him this and he will hand over the money." And then, as Santis turned toward Dumarest: "Don't bother to return for your friend—it would be a waste of time."

In the shadows a man was crying, "My arm! Dear, God, my arm!"

It had been slashed, cut to the bone, muscle and tendon severed from the vicious stroke of a blade. A cut which had won his opponent the bout and sent him circling the arena, smiling at the plaudits of the crowd. The man, now, was crippled and would remain so unless expensive surgery could be obtained to repair the damage. The skill was available—Dumarest knew the money was not.

He relaxed in the dimness, letting muscle and sinew unwind as he leaned back against the wall. For hours he had waited, acting the part of a dull, insensitive clod and the strain was beginning to tell. A normal man would have risen, walked about, done some limbering up exercises, at least had been curious as to what waited him, but he had been forced to do nothing but sit where he had been led and wait. Waiting he had listened. Listening he had learned.

Matpius, as he had guessed, was an animal wearing human shape. A dealer in flesh and blood to whom blood and pain came second to his reputation. A pander to the Cinque and those who could afford the best seats. His helpers were little better; sadists who enjoyed what they did. The bouts, as yet, had been normal enough; several for third-blood, some to the death, a couple for first-blood only. They had been for the benefit of those who prided themselves on admiring skill and not execution, the lovers of the quick parry, the lightning cut and thrust. An appreciation too fine for the majority who wanted to see more bloody action and who acclaimed as victor the man who could score three hits first. And even they paled against the feral demands of those who wanted nothing but a fight to the death.

Dumarest could hear them from where he sat; a screaming, shrieking ululation as if a horde of animals had scented prey. Men and women, shouting, yelling, eyes wide with blood-lust, nostrils flaring, hands clenched or tearing at their garments. The disgusting, the degenerate, the depraved.

Closing his eyes he could see them as he had so often before. See too the glitter of steel, the man holding the knife. The faces all looked the same; the visage of a beast lusting to kill, who had to kill in order to prevent being destroyed. The face of a creature intent on survival and revealing the primitive animal buried beneath the veneer of civilization.

A face matched by his own.

A gamble. Each time he fought in the arena it was a gamble. Not the calculated weighing of matched advantage but a blind, helpless dependency on the workings of chance. A pool of blood could cause him to slip and lose his balance and, in that moment, his life. A buried lump of excreta, a smear of oil, sweat falling to slick a surface. A badly adjusted spotlight the weakness inherent in the metal of his blade, his own nervous reaction to unexpected stimuli, all could cause his defeat. Things against which speed and skill were not enough. One day his luck would desert him. Today? Would it be today?

"Look alive there!" Delman came storming through the pens. "Get that mess cleaned up. Have the next contenders ready. You!" He glared at Dumarest. "Stand up, dummy!" He nodded as, woodenly, Dumarest obeyed. "Meat," he sneered. "But you'll serve. Ever used a spear? A net?"

Dumarest stood, staring, making no answer.

"You hold them one in each hand. With the net you trap and with the spear you thrust. You won't need that." He stooped to snatch the knife from where it rested in the boot, snarled as Dumarest dropped his hand to clamp fingers around the thick, hairy wrist. "All right, if that's the way you feel about it. Chonllen! Get this creep into position! Move!"

A gate led from the pens to the arena and Dumarest halted at the opening looking at the circling wall, the tiers of faces peering down from the stands. Rows of faces all blurred in the light streaming from the dome above, a clear brilliance stemming from artificial suns. The floor of the arena was thick with sand, tiny motes of silica catching and reflecting the light so that it seemed to watch with a host of dispassionate eyes. Facing him was another gate; a black mouth which yawned with hidden menace.

"Right." Chonllen handed him a spear and a net. "You go out there. You wait. When something comes at you you kill it. Do that and you win the prize. Five thousand on the clock but you lose ten kren for every second you delay." He pointed to where a wide-faced clock with thick, black hands rested against the far wall. "When the dial turns green the countdown starts. Luck!"

Dumarest moved forward into the arena, fumbling the net and spear, apparently clumsy and accentuating his poor coordination. An act to increase the odds against him and time for Kemmer to place his bets. Time too for him to gain the distance and examine his weapons.

The spear was broad-bladed, eighteen inches of edged and pointed steel set on a seven-foot shaft of polished wood. The net was of coarse mesh weighted at the edges with leaden pellets. A thing requiring skill to handle and Dumarest held it like a whip in his left hand, the spear poised in his right.

Beneath his boots the sand rasped like small clinkers, grains rubbing, edges honing one the other, the small sound more felt than heard.

Still the clock showed a white face.

Time, he knew, drawn out to increase the tension, to sharpen the anticipation of the crowd. Time too for him to assess the odds. To win anything at all he would have to kill whatever was sent against him within a few minutes. After eight he would be fighting for nothing except the chance to save his life. A desperate man would rush in, staking everything on the initial attack, trusting to surprise and speed to defeat his adversary. The net would be used to snare and hold, the spear to thrust—and the roar of the crowd would acclaim a classic victory. But such a man would be a fool.

Dumarest looked at the clock, still glowing with a nacreous lustre, then at the gaping mouth of the far gate. As yet he didn't know whom or what his opponent would be but he guessed it would be a beast, not a man. A man would have appeared by now, be moving, weaving in the preliminary dance heralding attack. The ritualistic but essential period when chances were calculated and position gained. When weaknesses were looked for and strengths observed. A moment loved by those who appreciated skill as well as blood.

A beast, then, but of what kind?

A bell rang with a sudden, nerve-numbing jar and, as the face of the clock turned green, nightmare came rushing from the gate.

In her seat Ellain Kiran turned, clutching at the arm of her escort, voice shrill with excitement as her fingers dug hard against flesh.

"Yunus! A sannak! And it's big! Big!"

Too big for any lone man to stand a chance against it especially a dull, half-witted creature such as had stood waiting. He turned, ignoring the pressure of the woman's fingers, looking for the plump man who had sought wagers. Kemmer was busy, picking his clients, firm as to the odds.

"My lord?"

"I back the beast. Will you take five to one against the man?"

"Seven would be better, my lord."

"Six." Yunus Ambalo was impatient. "Thirty against five in thousands. A deal?" He turned back to face the arena as

Kemmer nodded, confident the bet was as good as won. "And you, my dear? A thousand that the man falls within two minutes?"

"Accepted." She glanced at the clock then back at Dumarest. Suddenly, against all logic, she felt that he would win.

It was a confidence he didn't share. The creature was fast, sand pluming from beneath the long, tapered body as it writhed toward him. A moment to study detail and then he had sprung to one side, net lashing, spear levelled, the point rasping against a silicon-loaded hide as the beast turned and snapped with snouted jaws lined with flat, grinding teeth.

A thing from the desert. Life adapted to live even in the hostile environment of Harge. The body, snake-like, was segmented and scaled. The head was a conical projection split into the vise-like jaws. The eyes were covered with thick plates of transparent tissue. There was no observable ears, no feet, no neck, no weak points which Dumarest could recognize. Twelve feet long, three high, the creature was a mass of flexible sinew and iron-like muscle.

He jumped as the tail lashed toward him, landing to jump again, boots hitting the creature's back, gaining leverage to lift his body again in a long spring to one side. He'd turned in the air and landed, the net splaying from his left hand, the mesh badly aimed yet falling over the snout. Immediately he stabbed with the spear, the point glancing from the protective covering of an eye, skidding over the scaled carapace. An attack which took time and only his speed and agility saved his legs from been snapped by the vicious blow of the tail. Again he dodged, ran to the far end of the arena, ran again as the sannak writhed over the sand directly toward him.

The clock registerd the passing of forty seconds.

Four hundred kren clipped from the prize but Dumarest wasn't thinking of that. If he'd been the slow-moving clod he'd appeared he would be down by now, flesh and bone crushed by the sannak's jaws. No real contest and he wondered why Matpius had matched him against the beast. The answer lay in the avid faces ringing the arena; their desire for blood, the spectacle of butchery.

He jumped again, pluming sand rising to catch his throat and sting his eyes, grit sent to fog the air as the snake-like thing lashed itself forward with sweeps of body and tail. Again Dumarest lashed out with the net, snarling as the mesh failed to open, trying again then throwing it aside so as to leave both hands free to manipulate the spear. To face the creature was useless, scaled and protected it couldn't be harmed with the weapons he possessed, but if he could get behind it he might stand a chance. The scales would overlap and the spear could be thrust between them. Hurt, the thing could turn and expose its stomach and, if that was softer than its back, the contest would still be won.

A chime and the first minute had passed, a sound lost in the roar of the crowd as Dumarest jumped again, feeling the rasp of the lashing tail against the sole of his boot, landing to thrust the spear beneath a scale. Tissue held then yielded, green ichor welling from between the plates. A minor wound but on which convulsed the sannak so that, as if impelled by a spring, Dumarest rose high into the air, to turn, to land sprawling on the sand as his feet slipped on buried slime. A moment in which he was helpless and one in which the sannak attacked.

"God!" Ellain felt the contraction of her stomach, the chill which warred with mounting, sensual heat. "No! Dear God, no!"

She could see it now in imagination as she had seen it in reality before. The long snout thrusting, jaws parting, closing to the shriek of the victim, the crunch of bone. The jerk and then retreat as the severed limb was dragged free to be eaten while the hapless man watched blood jet from severed arteries to stain the stand. And then the rest, the crawling, the pleading, the terror and the final, horrible, slobbering death.

"No!" she cried again. "No!"

It almost seemed he heard her. Certainly he moved and with a speed which blurred his limbs so that one moment he sprawled helpless, the next he was standing, feet distant, the spear recovered and reflecting splinters of brilliance as again it thrust at the emerald stain on the scales.

"Clever," mused Yunus. "He's discovered a vulnerable point and is concentrating on it. A pity that he is wasting his time."

"Time," she said and looked at the clock. "You owe me a thousand."

A debt he acknowledged with a jerk of his head, his attention once again concentrated on the man and the beast in the arena. The creature had been made to bleed but from a point tough with inner sinew and flexible bone. A thing he knew but which the man could not. How long would it take him to change his pattern of attack?

The third bell and Dumarest realized he was doing nothing more than irritating the sannak. Backing, spear held before him, he reassessed the problem. The creature was armored, protected against winds and dust which could strip the surface of stone. It was at home in an environment in which no unprotected man could live for a minute. But no creature was totally invulnerable. Nothing alive was proof against injury and death.

He moved as again the snake-like body lunged toward him. Jumping he landed on the far side and noted how quickly the thing could turn. As it twisted the scales gaped, lifting to compensate, providing a target for anyone standing at the rear. Useless information; he was alone, what had to be done must be done by his own effort. Not the scales, then, and the stomach hugged the sand. The eyes were protected. The mouth?

It had to be the mouth.

He waited, taking his time, ignoring the clock, the chiming bell which registered the dimunition of the prize he didn't expect to win. It would be prize enough if he walked alive from the sand. A bonus if he remained unhurt.

"Move!" A woman screamed from the stands. "Attack, you coward!"

A soft and pampered creature who would fly into a panic at the slightest injury. One matched by a man who added his own insults, made brave by the comforting knowledge that he would never have to answer for his sneers. Dumarest ignored them as he ignored everything but the creature before him.

Like himself it had slowed down, the initial fury replaced by an instinctive caution. Strength and energy now had to be husbanded against the time of supreme effort when life and death hung in the balance and could be decided by an extra modicum of stamina. And yet it was a beast while he was a man. If it had the brawn he had the brain.

He tempted it, moving, retreating, the spear a darting irritation at the eyes, the jaws. Jaws which parted to snap, to miss, to snap again a little wider than before. To reveal a throat ridged and lined like the maw of the grinder it was. A target at which he stabbed, steel vanishing from sight, the point a lance which stung and was withdrawn, teeth rasping over the blade as Dumarest jerked it from between the jaws.

Again, green staining the polished metal. A third time and then, with a sudden rush, the thing was on him, following the point instead of withdrawing from it, the small but cunning brain learning from experience. Dumarest spun, the spear hampering his movements, throwing him off-balance as sand dragged at his feet. Holding him as the jaws parted to close like a vise on his boot just below the left knee.

"Earl!" Kemmer had seen and stood, stunned, his face was a mask of horror. "Earl!"

A cry lost in the thunder of the crowd rose, yelling, scenting the end. Once a sannak had hold the outcome was predictable.

But the jaws had closed on toughened plastic, not flesh, the material giving protection and winning time. Dumarest darted his hand down to his knife, whipped it from its sheath, thrust it edge upward between the jaws, the metal hard against his boot. Now, if they continued to close, the jaws would bite on edged steel, the blade serving to protect the limb. Before the beast could jerk its head and throw him to the floor Dumarest had slipped the shaft of the spear so as to rest against the knife, one hand on each side of the snout, parted, the left heaving while the right pressed down. Opposed leverage applied to the shaft resting between the jaws, wrenching them apart—if his strength was great enough, if the shaft would hold.

He felt the wood begin to bend, heard the crunch of teeth driving into the yielding material and strain harder, sweat running into his eyes, stinging, blurring his vision. Shortening his grip he applied the full strength of back and loins, snarling as the teeth dug deeper into the wood. If it broke, if the beast should think to throw him, if the knife should slip and his leg be crushed—it all depended on the shaft, his own determination, his own strength.

The clock chimed and was ignored. The crowd fell silent, watching, waiting, recognizing the precarious balance on which Dumarest's life rested. Then, as the knife fell from between the jaws, the silence was broken by a sigh. A sigh which rose to a shout as the boot was withdrawn from between the clamping teeth, a roar which thundered as, releasing the shaft, Dumarest sprang back, dodging the rush of the sannak, stumbling, recovering as he dived for his knife.

To rise with it in his hand, his only weapon now, the spear shattered, broken.

"Earl!" Ellain rose as she shouted the name she had learned from the plump man. Her trained voice was a shaft of searing brilliance in a turgid darkness. "Earl! My champion! Win, Earl! Win!"

He heard, ignoring the cry as he ignored the others, turning as he faced the beast, jerking back his head to save his eyes from a shower of grit flung toward him by the lashing tail.

A moment in which he glanced upward to see a shimmering flame of scarlet. The glory of hair caught in a vagrant beam and turned into a halo of unforgettable hue. Saw too the face shadowed beneath; the pale, almost translucent skin, the full slash of the generous mouth, the emerald pools of wide-set eyes.

Kalin!

A moment only and then he was facing the sannak again, knife poised, boots rasping the grit to gain traction. He saw the creature turn, the jaws gape and darted to one side as the thing charged. A maneuver repeated as he made his final play—to wear the beast down, to wait until it slowed, then to wound it again and again until, dead or hurt, it would give him mastery.

A plan which failed as, jumping to avoid a charge, he felt his foot slip, his ankle turning as he trod on a patch of buried slime. Then came the hammer-like blow of the tail which sent him slamming against the wall. The stars which burst in his eyes, the pain, the endless fall into darkness.

Chapter Four

Waking was a dream in which he rose slowly through layers of ebon chill, counting seconds, waiting for eddy currents to warm his body, electronic stimulus to activate his heart and lungs, drugs to eliminate the agony of returning circulation. A nightmare of traveling low, occupying a cabinet meant for the transportation of beasts, lying doped, frozen and ninety percent dead. Risking the fifteen percent death rate for the sake of cheap travel.

He had ridden like that too often, wondering each time if he would wake, welcoming each resurrection as it came.

Dreams. A plethora of faces which swam out of darkness to blur and vanish even as formed. One more stubborn which remained. A ghost with scarlet hair forming an aureole about a familiar face. The lips, the chin, the bottomless pools of the eyes. A sight which had started him, creating the moment of inattention which could have cost him his life.

Had he really seen her?

Could Kalin still be alive?

He turned, muttering, reliving old memories, old pain. Seeing again the woman he had known, the wonderful, beautiful thing she had been. Long gone now, vanished, only the gift she had given him remaining in his mind. The secret stolen from the Cyclan for which they hunted him from world to world. The key which would give them the domination of the galaxy.

"Dumarest!" The voice was dull, muffled. "Earl Dumarest!"

A voice backed by small, familiar sounds; a rustle of garments, of glass tapping against plastic, the soft susuration of a fan circulating air. A touch against his upper lip and acrid odors stung his nostrils.

"Dumarest. Wake up, man. Wake up!"

47

A command coupled with a reenforcing of his identity; standard practice when reviving a man who had been subjected to shock. Again the odors stung his nostrils, banishing the last shreds of sleep, but it was pleasant to lie and feel the pulse and surge of life. A comfort to stretch and feel the smooth embrace of sheets against his naked skin, the yield of a pneumatic mattress. The voice grew sharp with impatience.

"Can you hear me? Answer if you can. Answer!"

"I can hear you." Dumarest opened his eyes and looked at the face above his own. A young, smooth face, the features thinly precise, the eyes detached, the mouth a little too full but time would eradicate the hint of caring humanity. "How long have I been here, Doctor?"

The eyes blinked. "You are unusual. I would have bet you would have asked where you were."

"I know where I am. On Harge and this is a hospital. How long?"

"A day; an hour for diagnosis and examination, two hours slow time, the rest drug-induced sleep. How do you feel?"

"Hungry." To be expected—the two hours under slow time had accelerated his metabolism so that he had lived days in subjective time. Dumarest looked at his arms, noted the small, near-healed puncture in the hollow of one elbow. The mark left by intravenous feeding. "Glucose?"

"That and saline and a few other things. You had some cracked ribs, extensive bruising, slight concussion, torn muscles and strained ligaments. There is also minor kidney damage. The ribs had been treated with hormone glue to promote rapid healing and the kidney damage has been corrected. Just take things easy for a while and you'll be fine."

"How did I get here?"

"Carried by porters, I guess. The usual method. I only saw you after you'd arrived. Sit up now. Throw your legs over the edge of the bed. Dizzy? Bend your head down between your knees and it will pass. All right now?"

Dumarest nodded as he lifted his head. The nausea still remained in his stomach but the sudden giddiness and vertigo had gone. He looked at the instrument before his eyes.

"Hold steady now," said the doctor. "Just a final check. Look to the right . . . to the left . . . up . . . down . . . fine! Here!"

From a side table he lifted a container and removed the lid. Taking it Dumarest sipped and recognized the basic food of all spacemen; a compound thick with protein, sickly with glucose, tart with citrus and laced with vitamins. In space a cup was food enough for a day.

"Thanks." He handed back the empty container. "My clothes?"

"In that cabinet."

"My knife?"

"There too." The doctor looked appraisingly at the naked torso, the thin cicatrices of old wounds. "Just remember what I said and take things easy for a while." He took a card from his pocket, made check marks, signed and passed it over. "Take this to the desk in reception before you leave. They'll check you out. Don't forget to do it—the guards can be touchy."

"And the cost?"

The doctor shrugged, "I wouldn't know about that. The desk handles all matters of finance."

Reception lay at the end of a passage and contained a desk backed by enigmatic panels touched and graced with multi-hued points of light. A computer terminal, Dumarest guessed, one showing the occupancy of the hospital at all times together with full financial details. His eyes studied the place as he walked slowly toward the counter, the women in attendance. Reception was smaller than he'd expected, a few benches, some tables, a vending machine selling drinks and snacks. Doors bearing various numbers lined the walls and one, wider, the exit, was flanked by a pair of watchful guards. More, he was sure, would be stationed at the far end of the exit-passage, but it was worth a try.

"Your pass?" A guard extended a hand as Dumarest approached the door. He looked at the card the doctor had checked and signed. "This isn't a pass. Report to the desk and get proper clearance."

He watched as Dumarest obeyed, one hand resting on his belt close to a holstered weapon, his eyes suspicious. If the hard-faced woman who took the card had noticed the incident she made no comment. Feeding the card into a slot she busied herself with a keyboard, tore a slip from the print-out, attached it to a file and placed it before Dumarest.

"Sign on the bottom line, please." She watched as he scrawled his name. "Thank you. Here is your pass."

"Is that all?" He took the yellow slip. He had expected a bill and a large one. "How about the cost?"

"Payment has been taken care of, sir."

"By whom?"

"I am not at liberty to say." She added, blandly, "A friend is waiting for you in the outer hall."

It was larger than reception, lined with benches, each seat occupied with someone needing medical aid; a woman with a seared cheek, a man nursing a broken hand, a child with a face blotched with ugly sores. To one side sat a line of beggars, one with the gray of brain showing through plastic covering the hole in his skull. He held a chipped bowl in trembling, palsied hands. The label around his neck read; OF YOUR PITY HELP THIS MAN. The bowl was empty.

"Earl!" Kemmer stood beside the outer door, smiling, lifting a hand as he called. As Dumarest joined him he said, "It's good to see you. How do you feel?"

"Fine."

"Hungry? There's a place close to here which sells a decent stew. Cheap too as prices go. No?"

"No."

Food could wait. Dumarest led the way outside. The passage was wide, arched, the floor littered with benches; free seating accommodation provided by the hospital. Between them stood coin-operated diagnostic machines together with others selling a variety of drugs. Most were busy. Finding an empty bench Dumarest sat and, as the trader plumped down beside him, said, "What happened?"

Kemmer was direct. "You'd won the crowd, Earl. When you went down they yelled for your life. You'd been in for almost ten minutes and had put up a good show. They didn't want to see you killed—not when you couldn't put up a fight."

So he had been carried from the arena. "Did you pay for my treatment?"

"How could I?" Kemmer spread his hands. "You'd gone down, Earl. You'd lost." He added, bleakly, "We all lost. The money Carl got from Matpius, that we won betting, that we already had. All of it." He fell silent, brooding over the loss then said, "Didn't they tell you inside?"

"No." A problem but one which could wait. "Where's Carl?" He frowned at the answer. "In jail? Why?"

"It was when you went down," explained Kemmer. "The crowd was for you but the sannak wanted your blood. Carl jumped into the arena. He had a laser and used it. A disguised weapon—you know what mercenaries are. They feel naked without a gun. It stung the beast and sent it back to its den. Carl wasn't able to escape. The guards grabbed him and charged him with possessing an unregistered weapon within the city limits. They fined him a thousand kren."

The value Matpius had placed on a human life. Dumarest narrowed his eyes, thinking, seeing in imagination the old man jumping, staggering a little as he landed, rising to face the sannak with the laser his only defense. A small weapon it would have to be. Powerful enough to kill a man at close range but it could have done little more than singe the creature's scales.

He said, "We must get him released. Have you money?"

"A few coins. Enough for a meal or two but nothing more." He met Dumarest's eyes. If lying, he was convincing but, if lying, he would later be dead. A fact he recognized as he said again, urgently, "Earl, I swear it! I wouldn't hold out on you!"

Dumarest said, "Let's find out about Carl."

He was in a jail housed down a gloomy passage the walls polished and smoothed by the impact of countless bodies. Inside a desk faced a semi-circle of cells, each with a door pierced by a small grill, each with a number. Faces appeared at some of the grills as their footsteps echoed in the cavernous area. The smell was that of prisons everywhere; a combination of urine, excreta, sweat, stale air and disinfectant.

"Santis?" The officer in charge ran his finger down a list. Number eighteen. You come to pay his fine?"

"Not yet," said Dumarest. "What's the position?"

"Strangers?" The officer had the cold, searching eyes of a serpent. For a long moment he remained silent then, curtly, "He's got five days to raise the money. After that he starts collecting interest on his fine and cost of keep. His debt can also be sold to the highest bidder at open auction. To get free he has to clear it together with any accumulated interest. Compound, naturally."

"How much?" said Kemmer.

"Ten percent."

"A year?"

"A month. The standard rate." The officer pressed a button and, as the guard he had summoned came from the shadows, said, "This officer will show you out."

"Just a minute," said Dumarest. "What about his gun?"

"Confiscated."

Outside Kemmer drew in his breath and shook his head. "That about does it. I'd forgotten about the gun but it's not going to do him any good. Still, it was worth the try. Now what?"

Dumarest said, "We find Marta Caine."

She sat at a table following the dance of a small, white ball. One which skittered around the edge of a spinning wheel as her mind calculated the odds, the chance of its coming to rest on the red or black or the blank on which none were paid. Working the system which had first promised so much and which now was letting her down. And yet, with it, Corcyra had always won.

Against the squared baize she could see his face, one eyebrow lifted, the mouth quirked as if in secret jest. The face she had so often looked at as he lay beside her in the warm, soft bed, all passion spent, relaxed, finding time for the words he loved, the spells he wove with his endless tales. The secret he had imparted to her; he one which he swore enabled him to gamble and always win.

"Your bets!" The croupier stood with his hand on the wheel. "Make your bets!"

Time to make her move; a chip on the red, two on the black, one on low numbers, three on high. A spread which guaranteed nothing but the stretching of her resources yet which needed to be followed in order to eastablish the following wagers.

The wheel spun, the ball settled, came to rest. Black and high won and she felt relief as she scooped up her chips. Now for the next step and she waited as again the ball danced and again she won. Once more now, plunging deep, and then finish. Corcyra had been insistent on that. Three wins in a row and be satisfied—to continue was to invite ruin. And yet, when the luck was with her, it was hard to leave.

The decision was made for her by the settling of the ball and she watched, face impassive, as her chips were raked from the table. Now it was all to do again, to wait and watch and place small bets in an elaborate pattern. To calculate and try to ignore the tightening of her stomach, the mounting panic as luck went against her. Once she had thought Corcya weak—now she knew better. It took guts and courage to sit and risk the sum total of your resources in order to win enough to live on for a day. And then to return on the morrow and do the same. To follow the pattern, losing, still to play, still to follow the system when every nerve and sinew cried out in protest.

And, when winning, to know when to stop.

"Your bets! Place your bets!"

The ball bounced and settled and with a sigh of relief she scooped up her winnings and rose from the table. The net gain this time had been a little more than the last and far more than the disastrous one before, but she still lacked the security she craved. The bracelet she had pledged would have to stay with the jeweler as would her ring and the pendants she had worn in her ears.

"Marta!" Kemmer was heading toward her. "Marta, my dear, how nice to bump into you like this!"

She said, acidly, "Coincidence, Maurice?"

"No." He was bluntly honest. "I've been looking for you. We both have. Earl is downstairs. You weren't at home so we come looking."

"And found me." She moved farther from the table toward a shaded alcove where vending machines dispensed an assortment of drinks. A coin bought her a measure of water laced with alcohol and flavored with lemon. Kemmer joined her as she sat. "Unless you buy a drink you will be ejected," she warned. "You have money?"

"Not for luxuries. Could we walk?"

That at least could be done without charge but she was tired, the tables imparted a greater strain than was apparent, and she was in no mood to wander while he babbled. In no mood either to dispense charity but, as the attendant came edging toward them, she handed the trader a coin. To her surprise he handed it back.

"I'm not here for a handout."

"Then what?"

"Earl will explain." His face lightened as he looked past her. "Here he is now."

Dumarest carried a wrapped package beneath one arm. Setting it on the table, he fed coins into the vending machine, the watchful attendant moving away as he set drinks next to the package. To Kemmer he said, "Have you told her?"

"No."

"Told me what?" Marta looked from one to the other. "What the hell do you want?"

"Money." Dumarest was curt. "Carl is in jail and I want to get him out. You can help me. Don't worry—you won't lose by it."

"You're damned right I won't!"

"That is," he amended, "you won't lose if you cooperate." Casually he touched the package. "Did Maurice mention we looked for you at home? Just as well we did, in a way. Your door—"

"What about it?"

"Nothing." His smile was a mask. "A good, strong door," he mused. "Thumb-print lock too. Usually they're safe but you have to be careful to pull the panel tight when leaving. And even then there are ways—" He broke off, again touching the package, glancing at the busy tables. "Have any luck?"

"That's my business."

"I'm just asking." Dumarest took a sip of his drink. "You know, Marta, we're really in the same position. We all have to find some way of surviving while holding on to enough money to buy a passage on the next ship. Carl's been unlucky. So have you in a way. But if you were to lend Carl money to get out of jail you'd have not only a friend but an income. Interested?"

"I've got an income."

"The tables?" He shrugged. "Follow that route and there can only be one ending. Haven't you learned yet the one inescapable truth about gambling? That those who need to win never do?"

"Some—"

"Yes," he said. "We've all heard of the man who backed all he had on a throw of the dice and won and backed again and kept on winning until he owned a world. The woman who risked her child and ended by gaining freedom for all her tribe. The boy with nothing but his blood who ended with riches. And, of course, there are those who profess to make a living at the tables. Some do, I admit it, but not many and they are of a special type. Sensitives, the near-clairvoyant, those with some unusual talent. Others play the odds but only on games they can control. That wheel has no feelings. That ball obeys no laws. Neither can be bluffed. And the percentages are always with the house."

"Maybe."

"I'm offering you a certain profit."

She said, coldly, "I'm not interested. You go your way and I'll go mine."

"A pity." Dumarest half finished his drink and, again, his hand rested on the package: "I was thinking of your singing jewel. Here it would be a novelty if used correctly; demonstrated at private gatherings, for example, used to add a new dimension to a party or to entertain after dinner. You'd need guards, of course, to protect it. A thing like that could fetch a high price if offered in the right market. That is unless it was stolen first—you get my point?"

"You bastard!" She looked at the package, the same size as the box holding the jewel, remembered what he had said about the door—how else did he know the type of lock it had. "My jewel! You've stolen it!"

"Carl could be one of your guards, Maurice another. It would be safe then. And an agent could be found to find you work. But if you don't want to use it then I'll find another way." Rising he picked up the box. "Stay with her, Maurice. Don't let her call the guards until I'm well away."

"No!" Thought of losing the jewel made her feel sick. "You thief! You can't—"

But he could and would; his face told her that. Hard, firmly set, the mouth a thin, cruel line. A man intent on survival, a beast at war in a familiar jungle. And, once sold, the jewel would be lost. Her complaints would be ignored—who would care about a stranger?

"A loan," whispered Kemmer. "For God's sake, Marta, it's only a loan."

A stack of chips—she had them in her hand. Plastic discs convertible to cash against the loss of her jewel. "Here!" They rattled as she threw them on the table. "How much do you want? A thousand? Twelve hundred? Fifteen?" She watched as Kemmer scooped them up. "Now give me my jewel, you bastards! My jewel!"

"Maurice!" Dumarest waited until the man had gone. Quietly he said, "Your jewel is safe, Marta. I haven't got it, see?" Opening the wrappings he displayed a fiber carton. It was empty. "It's safe at home."

A trick. A bluff and for a moment she wavered between relief and anger. To have been taken in like a stupid child!

Her own fears turned against her, used as a weapon. She looked at the drink Dumarest placed in her hand.

"Get it down," he urged. "You'll feel better."

"You cheated me!"

"No," he corrected. "Pursuaded you."

"Tricked me. Conned me like an expert." As he'd promised, the drink had helped and, after all, what had she lost? "All that trouble," she said. "For an old mercenary. Why? What is Santis to you?"

"He saved my life." Dumarest found more coins as the attendant came moving again toward them. "Have another drink and I'll take you home."

Chapter Five

The day had begun badly with the new maid breaking an expensive flask of perfume. At midday a storm had seemed to be pending, dust swirling to settle after an hour, but the tension had remained, driving her to a casino there to lose more than was wise, to drink more than was good for the purity of her voice. And now this!

"Cancelled?" Ellain stared at the face in the screen. "You mean I'm not wanted?"

"Of course not!" Dell Chuba smiled his reassurance. "It's just that young Tage Helbrane has heard of a novelty and decided it would hold more appeal for his guests than yourself. A whim, of course, but you know what the young are. Once their curiosity has been satisfied you'll be back in favor."

Dropped because of a novelty! To the agent she said, "What is it this time? A singing jewel? Are you serious?"

He was and she had to accept it. As she had to accept the loss of a fee. And there could be further losses as the news of the thing spread. A bad time for it to happen with Yunus being so difficult. She reached for the phone, half-inclined to call him, then dropped her hand. It was no time to risk his displeasure and yet, now that the evening was ruined, what to do?

The maid had prepared her bath. Irritably she kicked a cushion from her path as she headed toward it. Naked, she slipped into the water, steam rising to condense in a mist of scented dew, the dew running down the mirrored walls in miniature rivers. A singing jewel! Before that it had been a harpist born with seven fingers on each hand, the extra digits giving him a unique mastery of the instrument. He had replaced a dancer of incredible flexibility who had ousted a juggler and before him had been—what? There had been so many. She couldn't remember.

57

The water broke into foam as she added perfumed chemicals, bubbles rising to break and rise again, each little explosion a tingle against her skin. A stimulation she enjoyed, one introduced to her by Yunus. He had been absent now for too long and she wondered if he had tired of her. She almost wished he had and yet, without him, how to survive?

Water splashed as she rose with impatient energy, small puddles marking where she had stood, droplets tracing her passage into the other room. The maid, eyes appraising, dried her and wrapped her nudity in a robe.

"Your hair, my lady?"

"Yes. After I've gone out, clean up and go." The girl shared a room in the servant's quarters. "I shan't need you until tomorrow."

As the girl started to dress her hair Ellain studied herself in the mirror. Still attractive, still superficially young, but already the small, telltale signs were beginning to show. The skin at the corners of her eyes held more lines than she liked. The cheeks, still firm, lacked a certain bloom. The chin, the set of the lips, the lines of her throat—all carried the subtle scars of time.

"You have beautiful hair, my lady." The maid's hands caressed the thick tresses as she guided the brush. "How shall I dress it? Casual? Formal? A crest or—"

"Casual." There was no need for an elaborate coiffure now that her appointment had been cancelled. "Just something simple. A chignon will do."

"And the gown?"

"No gown. Slacks and a tunic, one with a cowl." A choice dictated by a sudden decision. "Something suitable for the Stril."

If she wasn't to perform then she would watch while others did. Still restless she craved the anodyne of excitement. If nothing else she could watch the baiting or wander among the booths. Take a seat in the arena even—anything was better than just to sit and wait. And, perhaps, she would find adventure.

It was early but even so the area was busy with a life which ebbed but never died. The beat of drums merged with the thin wail of pipes and serpents wound sinuously over a naked, painted body. A man breathed fire and smoke, an ascetic displayed the skewers thrust into his flesh, a woman tittered and spun as she juggled glittering balls.

Before a booth a man threw knives.

He was tall, masked, naked to the waist, his torso marked with red and ugly wounds. His target was a young, dark-haired girl wearing a loose gown held by ties at shoulders and sides. She stood before a board, steel flashing to the clash of a cymbal, the knives thudding into the backdrop. Ties yielded as the blades severed the material, the gown opening to display a hint of the creamy skin and well-moulded body beneath.

Ellain watched with mounting fascination. How would it feel to watch a man hurl razor-edged steel at her naked body? To hear the hiss and thud as the point drove home? The sharp pain too, perhaps if it came too close. To cut and release blood. Had the girl ever been hit? Had any died?

"A sample," roared the barker. "Come inside and see more. Watch as the girl is stripped naked, facing death to be held in a cage of steel. See how a fighter trains. Try your luck at beating a champion with no risk of injury to yourself. Learn how to throw a knife and use a living man as a target. Hit him and win a hundred kren. Hurry! Hurry! Hurry!"

Yielding to a whim, Ellain joined the crowd thrusting money at the woman selling tickets, the girl's mother, she guessed. Inside she took a place close to the wall away from a raised platform. The place quickly filled. In a short while the girl, again completely covered, entered and took her position against a board. The man, still masked, followed. A clash of cymbals and the performance began.

The owner watched with mounting satisfaction. Business was good and would get better as the word passed and the young bloods came to try their luck. He'd been wise. Dumarest was everything he claimed and had done exactly as he promised. Knife-throwers were common enough but he'd added the unusual. To offer himself as a target had seemed to be inviting suicide but, as yet, he'd not been touched. The apparent wounds were nothing but paint, bait for the gullible to try their luck.

And, at a score of kren a time, few could resist the temptation.

Again the cymbals and Gillian stepped from the ring of blades, naked, untouched and smiling. A good girl and one dear to his heart as she was to her mother's. One with courage and, he was afraid, more than a casual interest in the new attraction. A situation which could lead to trouble unless handled delicately but, in the meantime, money was to be made.

He moved forward, announcing the next part of the program, stepping back as Dumarest went through ritual motions; the hold, the cut and stab, the parry, the attack. A short and basic demonstration of fighter technique which fullfilled the promise and whetted the appetite for what was to come. He moved into the crowd as Dumarest showed how to hold a blade, to poise and throw it, taking his time as the owner sold tickets and collected money. In the Stril time was of value. A show had to be short, sharp and cleanly ended. Once the punters had been milked they had to be got rid of so as to make room for more.

The cymbals again and the last part of the program commenced. Dumarest, armed with a short metal bar in each hand, stood with his back to a loosely hung section of fabric. He faced the crowd and Ellain saw the glitter of his eyes through the holes in the mask as he looked at her. The robe she wore was the color of her hair. The cowl was raised.

"And now," said the owner, "a chance to hurt. To kill and to win a hundred kren. Throw your knife, hit the man and collect. You first, sir."

A youth, trembling with eagerness, stepped forward. Awkwardly he threw the knife handed to him, the blade turning, the weapon hitting sidewise against the loose fabric as Dumarest stepped aside.

"And you, sir. Then you. And you." The owner passed out knives. "One at a time, now, but hurry!"

A big man, smiling, confident, sent his blade hurtling through the air. It was parried by a deft swing of one of the metal bars. Another, deflected, buried its point in the floor. More followed, a dozen, a score, then as men clamored for further chances the owner called a halt.

"That ends the show, ladies and gentlemen. Another will begin in a few minutes. If you wish to try your luck again return and you are welcome to do so. This way out, please. Hurry! Hurry! Hurry!"

Hurry and leave to talk and return and pay again to enter. An extra charge at the door added to the fee for using the knife. Ellain lingered until she was the last conscious of the masked man's stare.

She said, "There will be a note waiting for you with the woman who sells tickets."

One written on paper bought from a vendor, sealed with scented wax, given with money into the woman's hand. A note she was certain would bring him at midnight to her door.

The recording was of Dowton's *Transpadane*, a clever enough composition but one lacking true depth of artistry, though the blended voices of the chorus and duet held a certain charm. She muted it as the bell announced a caller, checking the exterior before opening the panel, throwing it wide to stand haloed by the light from the room behind.

"Well!" She backed as Dumarest lifted his hands toward her. "So impetuous! But, at least, you are on time."

He followed her into the room, annoyed at his own reaction. It had been a trick of the light, the color of the hair now cascading in a thick tress over one shoulder, the golden tunic which ended at mid-thigh to leave the long column of her legs in full view. A coincidence. The possibility of anything else was too remote. Yet even so he had to ask.

"Did you originate on Solis?"

"Solis?" Smiling, she shook her head. "No. Why do you ask?"

"You resemble someone I knew who lived there. The color of your hair is a planetary trait."

"You like it." Spinning she caused it to lift and spread. "I'm glad. But my world is Nyadoma. And yours?"

"Earth."

"Earth?" She added, surprised. "That's odd. I've a friend who mentioned it once."

Dumarest said, carefully, "This friend of yours—could I meet him?"

"Perhaps. Of course he could have been joking. It's an unusual name for a planet. Forget him now. Some wine?"

She poured without waiting for an answer, handing him a goblet half-filled with fluid the color of blood. Drinking she watched him, studying his face, his eyes, the set of his lips, the plane of his jaw. She hadn't been mistaken; the masked man in the booth was the same one who had faced the sannak.

She smiled when he admitted it. "I knew I was right. But what makes a fighter like you waste his skill in a cheap booth? Money? You get a share of the take?" Then as he nodded. "And the girl? Do you share her too?" She shrugged as he made no answer. "You could do better, Earl. Much better."

And perhaps she would help him. Her note had mentioned the possibility of financial gain; shrewd bait to attract a desperate man. And who else would expose himself to thrown knives?

She said, "You're trying to build a stake so as to back yourself again in the arena. The reason for the mask—you want to hide your skill. But it won't work. You are known now and no one in his right mind would be willing to face you. Certainly no one would bet against you. One of the penalties of a small world."

He said, dryly, "But not the worst."

"No." She drank, wishing he hadn't mentioned it, and yet it gave them a common bond. "Debt," she said. "On Harge the route to hell. And one so easy to take. I arrived with the conviction I would achieve fame and wealth. My singing would entrance all who heard it and they would laud me and my reputation would flower. A mistake—here there is no great auditorium and little surplus wealth for the majority to spend. An error compounded by another when I stayed instead of leaving when I had the chance. And I have always been a poor mathematician." Pausing she asked, bitterly, "Have you any idea of how quickly a debt can mount?"

"On Harge it will double in seven months and treble in a year."

"Unless the interest is paid. If not it will mount to ten times as much in two years. Ten times!" This time when she drank she emptied the goblet. "All I earn, everything I get, barely does more than pay the interest on what I owe. And until the debt is paid I can't leave. I'm not permitted to pass through the gate when a ship is on the field. I'm trapped! A prisoner chained for life!" Then, with a sudden change of tone she added, lightly, "Unless, of course, I can find someone to give me help. Someone like you."

"Give?"

"An unpopular word," she admitted. "But the help would be mutual."

He said nothing but looked around the apartment, at the soft furnishings and ornaments of price. She guessed he thought her a liar.

"This place isn't mine, Earl. It belongs to Yunus Ambalo

and he is of the Cinque. They own Harge. Yunus thinks he owns me. I have an objection to being regarded as property."

"You could leave," said Dumarest. "You don't have to accept his charity."

The truth, but as unpalatable now as ever. Ellain thought of the alternatives and said, unsteadily, "It isn't as simple as you make it sound. Yunus owns my debt and can be vindictive. Until it's paid—" She broke off, shaking her head, reaching for the decanter. Light glowed from the ruby stream as she refilled her goblet. "I need help, Earl. Not a sermon."

"You think I can give it?"

"I'm sure of it." She came to join him, pushing him on a couch, sitting at his side, one long thigh pressed against his own. Her hair swirled a little as she turned to face him. The scent of her perfume was the cloying odor of lilies. "I watched you when you fought in the arena and even Yunus had to admit you were far above the average. You have speed, strength, can use your brains and watch for advantage."

"I lost."

"Because something happened. What? I remember that you turned and looked at me just before you went down. Was I the cause?" Her full lips parted in a sensuous smile. "Did I stun you with my beauty? Say I did, Earl. Even if it isn't true it would be nice to hear you say it."

A child begging for compliments but, no, she was far from being a child. Seated close as he was he could see now that any resemblance to Kalin was due to the hair, the soft focus of distance. This was a woman who had lived hard and long, one who needed artifice to maintain her youthful appearance. The bones were good, the carriage, but the skin and the tissue beneath betrayed the passage of time.

She said, frowning, "Earl, what are you looking at?"

"Your beauty, Ellain." It was politic to lie. "You are very beautiful."

She smiled and, suddenly, he was no longer a liar. Her beauty still remained, waiting to flower when she relaxed and ceased to act the part she had chosen to play. But even so something lingered. A shadow, the trace of some interior warping which colored her attitude to life and dominated her reaction to events. A thing he had seen before in the eyes of jaded women who had screamed lewd invitations when, victorious, he had walked from the arena.

"Earl, you are so much a man." Ellain rested her fingers on his hand, letting the tips caress his skin. "So wonderfully primeval. A human governed by an animal's simple creed. To eat in order to live. To kill in order to eat." Her voice thickened as she edged closer. "Have you killed often, my dear? Tell me how it feels to kill."

Talk and feed her imagination, stimulating it with thoughts of blood and pain, of combat and wounds and final victory. Triggering her sexual drives so as to render her a willing victim to an ancient domination.

He said, "Is that what you want me to do? To kill Yunus Ambalo."

"What?" The suggestion was sobering, frightening, but even so it held an attraction. Yunus lying on her floor, dead, ripped, bleeding—madness! "No! No, of course not!"

"A mistake. I apologize."

"You should. It was insane even to suggest it." More softly she added, "Would you kill him if I asked?"

"No." Dumarest was blunt. "I'm not that stupid. To kill one of the Cinque would be to invite an unpleasant end."

"One more horrible than you imagine. And it would do no good. His heirs would inherit my debt and I'd still not be free." Her fingers resumed their caress. "Why aren't you drinking? Isn't the wine to your liking?"

It was rich, holding tartness, a hint of an astringent pungency. He drank, holding the fluid in his mouth, tasting, wondering what she could have added to the original brew.

"You're suspicious," she said, watching him. "Earl, you're so suspicious. Have other women invited you to their homes? Tried to drug you? Used chemical artifice to pursuade you to their beds?" Her laughter held a genuine amusement. "Am I so old that I need take such measures? So ugly that I must delude a man into becoming a lover?" Rising she turned, arms uplifted, the thrust of her breasts prominent against the shimmering gold of her tunic. Her hips and thighs were a poem in seductive curves. "Shall I sing for you? Would you like me to sing?"

Without waiting for his answer she crossed to the player, changed the recording, stood poised as music welled from the speakers. A raw, nerve-scratching pulse of drums mingled with the sobbing of pipes, the wail of a lonely flute. Her voice matched the piece; yearning, calling, stimulating an inherent, primitive response so that Dumarest was acutely aware of her proximity, the feminine scent of her body, the aching need of her flesh.

Aware too of the trap into which she was leading him. Tantalizing him with a lure as old as time. As the piece ended he said, bluntly, "Did you ask me here just to provide an audience?"

"You think it such a small thing? For that one song alone I have been paid—" Her anger dissolved in sudden recognition of the absurdity of what she was saying. But still her pride needed to be appeased. "Are you saying you didn't enjoy it?"

"My lady, I enjoyed it too much. And I drink to your talent!" Deliberately he emptied the goblet. To insult her more would be worse than stupid. And, though he recognized the transparent attempt at seduction, she had what he needed; the possibility of money and a friend who knew of Earth. Casually he mentioned him adding, "What does he do?"

"Hunt, I think. You are eager to meet him?" She read the answer in his eyes and recognized the advantage it gave. "It could be arranged."

"When?"

"Perhaps tonight. It's possible he will be at Tariq Khalil's party. Another novelty." Her eyes darkened at memory of the slight. "I should have performed but would be welcome as a guest and you can be my escort. Why not?" She smiled, anger forgotten. "Amuse yourself, Earl, while I change."

The room reflected its owner; delicate, fussy, spoiled. Dumarest moved around, looking, halting before an image which sat, grimacing with endless pain. Another depicted a scene in the same mode; a couple this time locked in an embrace which blended ecstasy with torment. Gifts from Yunus?

He moved to the player and changed the recording, picking a crystal at random, the throbbing of strings echoing his choice. The air was warm, tainted with a peculiar odor and he guessed that spices had been burned to provide a pungent incense. From the bedroom he could hear small sounds as the woman busied herself. Moving away from the door he reached the masked window. A button cleared the panel.

Under the blazing light of massed stars the desert looked like a frozen, silver sea.

It was calm now, the air free of wind, the undulating dunes locked in a transient stasis. One which held a unique beauty for never again could the sand take on that same exactitude. The shape and flow of the ridges would be changed, the shallow dells, the peaked mounds, the long, sensuous slopes which seemed to reach to eternity. Then, at the limit of vision, looming like a toothed ridge against the glow of the sky, rested a long range of uneven mounds.

"The Goulten Hills," said Ellain. "In time they too will be desert."

She had come to stand at his side, moving soundlessly on naked feet, her hair lifted and bound with a golden fillet the scarlet strands drawn up tight against the round perfection of her skull. A thick, fluffy robe enveloped her and her face, wiped free of cosmetics, looked startlingly young in its innocence.

A trick of the light; the silver glow from beyond the window was kind. Or an inner relaxation so that now, for the first time, Dumarest saw her as she really was. A child trapped in a woman's body and forced to live in a harsh, adult world. Then, looking beyond her, he saw the images and their depiction of endless pain. No child—or if so one who had more than her share of childish cruelty. He recalled the faces he had seen edging the arenas in which he had fought—they too, at times, could look innocent and young.

"It can be beautiful at times," she whispered, looking at the desert. "The storms come and the world changes and everything vibrates to the fury of the wind. You can hear it screaming as if it's a thing alive. Watching it, you can imagine eyes, a mouth, hands reaching to rend and tear, claws to rip. A destroyer awful and magnificent in its terrible power."

"Wind," said Dumarest. "Sand and dust. There's nothing else."

"No?"

"Creatures, perhaps." He thought of the sannak. "An adapted form of life."

"And ghosts," she said. "Never forget the ghosts. I dream of them at times; those caught in the storms, the others condemned to die in them. The old, the helpless, those so deeply in debt there can be no prospect of them ever getting clear. Those who refused to pay—have you never thought of that, Earl? Wondered how they are dealt with? The Cinque have found a way."

Murder—to expose anyone unprotected to the winds would be nothing else. Legalized, perhaps, justified on the grounds of logic, but murder just the same.

"That's why I've got to get away," said Ellain. The mask of the window rasped across the pane as she pressed the button. "I dream of it at times. Of being out in a storm, lost, hopeless, doomed. To be flayed and, still living, to crawl while the flesh is stripped from my bones. To be skinned, blinded, turned into a thing of horror. God! Earl, I can't bear to think of it!"

"Then don't!"

"To be driven out, left to wait, to watch." Her voice rose, became a scream. "To—Earl! Don't let it happen! Don't—"

She broke off as he slapped her cheek, a gentle blow but one hard enough to quell her incipient hysteria. As she lifted her hand to the mark of his fingers he fetched her wine.

"Drink this."

"Earl?"

"Drink it and stop worrying. No one is going to turn you out into a storm."

Not yet, perhaps not ever, but the threat was always present. Wine slopped as she drank, a ruby stain appearing on her chin, another on her robe. Dumarest took the empty goblet she handed to him.

"Earl, I'm sorry."

"For what?"

"For acting the fool. I didn't come out here to make an exhibition of myself. It was just seeing the desert and you and hoping you could get me away from here—am I asking too much?"

He said, harshly, "You're saying too little. If you have a plan tell me what it is. I need data to work on, facts, information. I can't promise a miracle."

"But you'll do your best? You won't forget me?"

"No." He mastered his impatience. If she offered nothing then he was no worse off than before. And there was always her friend. But to press was to betray his eagerness and to do that was to risk too much. "Hadn't you better get ready now?"

"Yes." She stepped back and took a step toward the bedroom then turned, one hand plucking at her robe, the fabric parting to reveal the smooth sheen of her skin. She was, he guessed, naked beneath the garment. "I came to suggest that you could use the shower if you wanted. Take a bath, even."

"Thank you."

"I just thought that after your work at the booth—" Her

gesture was expressive. "And as we're going to a party, well, you understand."

He had bathed before calling and he understood too well. But it suited him to play her game, to strip and stand beneath a flood of scented water, to dry himself, to step into the bedroom and to see her, waiting. To take her. To hold her close, the robe falling, her naked flesh pressed hard against his own. To feel her demanding heat and his own, urgent response. To lift her on the wide, soft bed and there to remember another time, another place when hair the color of flame had burned no brighter than his passion.

Chapter Six

Tariq lived high in the Khalil Tower, his private apartment fitted with windows, a covered walk, a place from which to look at the distant hills but lower, where he held his select gatherings, there were no windows. Instead, to make the affair a success, there were drifting globes which burst to emit puffs of colored smoke, others which gave birth to acrid scents, subtle perfumes, noxious odors. Shimmering membranes snowed the air each singing with whispers, murmurings, sonorous chords, lewd suggestions, jokes, ribaldries.

The wine was touched with rainbows, the food a plethora of shape and form; miniature ships, cities, castles, naked men and women, obscene monsters, beasts, things from the nightmare of imagination all resting on salvers decorated with slowly moving fringes of pseudo-life. Jellies shook and pulsed to subsonic rhythms and strobes froze hectic movement in transitory chiaroscuros. There was an acrobat, a dancer, a man who performed illusions. A mutant with a twin growing from his side. A man who wrung magic from a guitar. An old woman with a singing jewel.

There was no time in Harge. Only a window could tell the passing of day and night; the rest was a constant glow dulled only by intent. Life progressed at a steady pace, hours rolling one into the other, natural divisions blurred into a matter of convenience. But Marta Caine had her own biological clock and she was tired.

It was an ache which seemed to have penetrated her very bones so that she sat, back against the wall, the box holding the jewel cradled in her lap. Beyond the wall of the small room the party throbbed with undiminished energy, a sound which grew louder, to fade as the door was closed.

"Marta?" Kemmer was standing before her, a frosted glass of wine in one hand, a plate of dainties in the other.

69

"Marta?" He smiled as she opened her eyes. "Here, drink this wine and have a bite of food. It will help restore your strength." His smile masked concern. "Come now. They may call for you soon."

Never would be soon enough the way she was feeling but she made an effort, tasting a little of the food, gulping the wine. Santis reached his hand on her own as she made to set down the plate.

"Eat. Maurice, some more wine?" As the trader left he said, with unexpected insight. "The jewel?"

"Yes." The lid of the box lifted beneath her hand. "It gives," she murmured. "But also it takes." The dull surface was smooth to her touch. "Its beauty needs to be fed."

With more than the ultraviolet light supplied by the lamp she had bought; the chemical sprays with which she moistened its facets. Each time it sang it robbed her of a little more of her strength; giving and taking even as it gave. A symbiote needing the proximity of her humanity and taking nervous energy in return for the mood it created.

"You've been working too hard," said the mercenary. "Too many performances too soon. After this you rest for a few days. I'll have a word with Dell Chuba when I collect the fee." He forced lightness into his tone. "Now eat up, my dear. It all helps."

Sustenance which was as good as money and she forced herself to eat the spiced and pungent morsels. The plate was almost empty when Kemmer returned bearing a full decanter.

"This should last us," he said. "The best—they can afford it. I thought we might as well take the opportunity while it was going. I guess we won't be kept waiting much longer."

"How is it out there?"

"As you'd expect." He smiled at her as he refilled her glass. "Noise, talking, dancing—how else do the rich enjoy themselves?" Casually he added, "I saw Earl while I was getting the wine."

Santis said, "Alone?"

"No. With the red-haired woman who shouted to him in the arena. She's got money from the look of her. Maybe Earl's trying to get back some of that five thousand her escort took off us when he went down."

"Or maybe he's just making the most of an opportunity."

"That could be it," agreed the trader. "Making contacts, finding out who can do what—that's half the battle. More than half if the truth be told. And advertising covers the rest. Once known, get yourself talked about. Make yourself appear to be important. People always want what they think is rare or valuable."

Marta Caine said, thoughtfully, "Earl needs to be careful. If that woman has a wealthy lover he could turn awkward. It would be simple for him to hire an assassin."

"A risk," admitted the mercenary. "But life is full of risks and no man can avoid them all."

Least of all himself, she thought as, sipping the wine, she watched him drink from the decanter. Like herself he was old and must also be tired but if he was, no sign showed on the seamed face or in the hooded eyes. But his weariness would be the natural result of physical strain while hers came from a deeper source. How long, she wondered, until she had nothing left to give? Would the jewel then fail to respond? And, if it did, what then?

She knew the answer yet hated even to consider it. To pass the jewel on to another; to lease it out. To provide it with a young a vibrant counterpart. Yet the jewel was hers, a part of her life, a thing too personal to be handed on like an old shoe. And what if it preferred the new stimulus and failed to respond ever again to herself?

A worrying thought and she pushed it away from her as she had always managed to push away troublesome things—a trick she had learned long ago when to brood over misfortune would have been to invite insanity. One taught her by an old harlot willing to teach a younger colleague how to survive the black and evil emotions haunting the profession.

To think, when depressed, of bright things; the fees which were mounting and the security they represented. Of the safety provided by the guards. Dumarest had been right and she had to admit it.

What was he doing here? Scheming, planning, waiting for opportunities? The presence of the woman was obvious and she felt a momentary envy of the embrace she had known or would experience, Once she too had felt the ecstasy to be found within a man's arms. Which she could feel again if only the right man would make himself known. Someone like Corcyra or Dumarest—odd how they both shared so many of the same characteristics.

"Marta!"She started as Santis touched her shoulder, conscious that she had dozed. "You'd better check your appearance," he advised. "You could be summoned any moment."

Alejandro Jwani was slimly built, of medium height, his head peaked, balding, the ears highly convoluted. His hands were small, delicate, the nails blunt and polished. His clothes were touched with vivid colors at wrist and throat; flashes of scarlet and lemon showing bright against a dull purple. Ellain's friend and if he knew anything of Earth he was reluctant to admit it.

"A name," he said. "One which intrigued me a little. Would you care to try one of these exotic delights?"

Dumarest looked at the tray held before him, selected a harmless seeming cone topped with a violet crystal, bit into it and tasted vileness.

"You lost," said Jwani handing him wine. "I could tell it from the way you puckered your mouth."

The wine helped but the taste still lingered. Ellain, smiling, offered him a triangle coated with sparkling dust.

"Here, Earl, this is sweet, I promise. Unless, of course, Tariq has changed the culinary pattern since his last assembly."

He hadn't, the morsel was sweet and eliminated the lingering foulness of the cone. Dumarest said, "Ellain mentioned you were a hunter, Alejandro. On Harge?"

"You are wondering what there could be on this world to hunt, Earl. Am I right? And yet do not be misled by a word. To hunt—what does it mean? To look for, to search, to engage on a quest, to seek—how meaning can change. This dish now." Jwani lifted the plate. "Each morsel is a gamble and to find one which is palatable is surely to hunt for sweetness?"

"Or to hunt for vileness."

"True and again you demonstrate how meaning can alter. All words are but labels and each can be read in more than one way. Good, bad—good as compared to what? Bad as compared to what? And, if there is no good, can there be anything which is bad? Anything which is evil? You recognize the problem, my friend?"

The man was more than a little drunk despite his apparent sobriety. Any meaningful communication would have to wait. Dumarest took the plate from Jwani's hands and set it on the table. Stimulated by the disturbance of air, the warmth of his flesh, tendrils of pseudo-life lifted to wave like blind and seeking worms.

"I have offended you," said Jwani. "You are offended."

"There can be no offense where there is no intention to offend." Dumarest reached for a decanter and poured a stream of scintillant wine into a goblet shaped and colored like a rose. "I merely freed your hands so as to give you this." He placed the goblet into the empty hands. "So as to offer you a toast with this." He lifted his own glass. I drink to your health!"

"Good or bad?"

"Good, naturally. Are you my enemy?"

Jwain said, dryly, "From what I've heard of you, Earl, it wouldn't be healthy to be that. Rest assured I am your friend."

"And friends should meet. Tomorrow?"

"Tomorrow. Later, certainly. Ellain knows where I am to be found. And now—" He swayed a little, his face turning suddenly black. "And now I think I need a . . . a little. . . ."

Dumarest caught him as he fell. Attendants, answering Ellain's signal, came rushing to relieve him of the burden. As he made to follow them from the room she caught his arm.

"No, Earl!"

"He needs help and—"

"But not from you. Understand me, Earl, it's a matter or pride. The servants don't matter but if he knew you had seen him ill, vomiting, at his worst, he would never want to face you again. He would even take your presence as a deliberate insult. Believe me."

She had no reason to lie and it sounded reasonable. Certainly he had run into stranger mores but it was a chance lost. Few men when in need would be reluctant to accept help and, when drunk, a man often could be influenced to tell more than he intended.

Ellain said, "I'm sorry, Earl. If Alejandro has a fault it's that he can't hold his liquor. He also doesn't know when to stop. Usually he just becomes a bore but tonight he outdid himself. Still, it gives you an advantage."

"How?"

"He doesn't usually remember just what he's said toward the last." She looked at him without expression. "Shall we dance?"

He led her to the center of the floor, her scarlet hair cascading over an emerald gown, her waist caught with a cincture of gold, more gold hugging her naked, high-arched feet. Dumarest had little interest in the dance but the needs of the arena had made him light on his feet and the beat of the music was easy to follow. Ellain matched his movements, accentuating them, adding more of her own so that she spun like a tinted river against the gray of stone. A display overpraised by a sharp-eyed woman with a painted face and nails which would have suited a feline.

"My dear, you were superb! It's such a comfort to your friends to discover you can do more than sing. I was distraught when I learned you were not to entertain us—but there are consolations."

"Of course, Weenedia. That of attending as a guest for one. I no longer have to pretend to be amused by ignorance."

The woman ignored the insult. Her voice was acid. "A new friend, I see?" Her eyes glanced toward Dumarest. "I wondered what had happened to Yunus, then I remembered he was engaged with the Barroccas on a matter of cost adjustment. Have you met Ieko Barrocca? A sweet and fantastically lovely young woman. I'm sure they will be very happy. Ah! I see young Tariq over there. I think he is about to entertain us with his new novelty."

"Bitch!" Ellain stared after the woman as she hurried away. "Trust her to turn the knife!" And trust her to tell Yunus of the dance and of Dumarest. Well, to hell with him. For tonight at least. If he was with the Barroccas he wouldn't be bothering her. And the dance had made her acutely aware of her body. "Earl, I'm bored. Take me away from here."

"Now?"

"Why not? Alejandro has left and we've done what we came for. We could walk in the gardens or visit the gymnasium. See some baiting or try a sensatape. Or we could just go back home." Her eyes told him which she preferred. "There'll be no need to hurry now. We can talk and make plans. Earl?"

Before he could answer the air trembled to the clash of a gong and, with suitable solemnity, Tariq Khalil presented the singing jewel.

Marta Caine had changed, Dumarest could tell it at once as, dressed in a long, flowing gown of sequined black, she walked from the side room out into the center of the floor. Carl and Maurice attended her, both wearing robes, the trader bearing the now-decorated box, the mercenary watchful, as always on guard against a sudden rush, a snatch, a threat to the jewel or its owner.

"This is nonsense!" Ellain didn't trouble to lower her voice. "Stupid theatricallity. What the hell's she supposed to be? A priestess of some kind?"

Dumarest said harshly, "She is a woman trying to earn a living. Respect that if nothing else."

"But—"

"Damn you! Shut up and give her a chance!"

She fell silent, shaken by his fury, wondering at his concern for a stupid old woman who walked with hands lifted in supplication as if she were praying. A woman both old and ugly; the ebon veil covering her hair framed a living skull.

Time, she thought, it brings this to us all. Age, the insidious poison which robs flesh of its firmness, muscle and tissue of resiliency. She remembered what she had seen in her mirror and felt a sudden revulsion. No! Better to die than to linger to look like the poor creature now standing, hands extended for the box which the robed figure extended toward her. The box she touched and the lid she slowly lifted while, from the musicians, came the solemn beat of a muffled drum.

Theatrical buffoonery—but effective. Even she felt the growing tension. The intangible feel of something stupendous and terrifying about to happen—a tension which mounted as the aged hands dipped into the box to lift, cupped, to poise while the fingers slowly opened to reveal what they contained.

"Glass!" She whispered her disappointment. "By God, it's just glass!"

"No." Dumarest answered her. "Not glass. Now be silent and watch what happens."

The drumbeat continued, fading, dying as if retreating to make way for something new and marvelous; becoming a stirring whisper as, its heraldry accomplished, it stole quietly from the scene.

To leave silence.

A silence which lengthened until the ears seemed to ache with waiting and then, slowly, so slowly, the jewel began to brighten, to illuminate the skeletal fingers caressing it, the skeletal face behind it. A face which tilted as the hands lifted the jewel. One which became transfigured as the gem began to sing.

And, in the song, was death.

A dirge which keened the end of all life, all sunsets, all dawns. A thin, whining threnody which told of the chill and empty places between the stars, of ice, of deserts, of hopeless emptiness. Of the slow and inevitable halting of growth and the termination of desire.

Depression came to kill the party. A cloud of endless night which froze the smiles of anticipation and converted jovial congress into the strained facade of a wake. In imagination faces became skulls and fleshless jaws gaped in grimaces which were the mockery of smiles.

"No!" Ellain felt the constriction of her stomach, her heart. "Dear God, no!"

The *Interlude* had never been like this. Ecuilton's despair had never touched such depths. Even Schiller in the madness which had created the *Tubero* had failed to induce such hopeless resignation. She felt smothered by it. Condemned and yet accepting the condemnation. Dying and resigned to death. Seeing the approaching termination of her entire existence and, singing, accepting it. Dying as she sang. Singing as she died.

No, not her—*it*!

The thing cradled in the thin, bony fingers. Or was it the fingers which sang and the glowing jewel only amplified? Or the woman whose hands they were? Or the brain behind the skull-like face? Or the mind within the brain? The soul? The intangible something which could never be seen, touched, measured, felt. The ego. The individual.

Not her—*it*!

An enemy, robbing her of life, of hope, of love. Taking all she held of value. A thing of crystal, glowing, singing, singing—and if she could do nothing else she too could sing.

Sing as the jewel sang, her voice rising, keening, the tone modulated to near-perfection, stomach and lungs, throat and larynx, mouth and teeth and lips and tongue all amplifying and directing and harmonizing the throbbing of the column of air she had created.

The note.

The rising, singing, vibrating note which rose to shrill, to merge with the song of the jewel, to blend with it, to resonate with it, to find the key, the harmonic of the stone itself.

Unseen, unheard, glass shattered on the tables and a woman screamed as she clutched her ears. A scream repeated as another fell, followed by a youth, a man, another girl. Dumarest felt the pain stab his eardrums and lifted his hands, palms cupped to give protection. Muffled as it was, the sound still penetrated and he saw Marta's face, the blood seeping from her nostrils, the lobes of her ears.

And still Ellain, mouth wide, throat corded with effort, sent the magic of her voice to challenge that of the jewel.

She had broken glass as a girl, won bets on her ability to do so, even ruined a crystal chandelier in the auditorium on Weem—an accident and one never repeated but she still had the power. And now, more than ever before, she used it. Seeking, altering her tone a fraction at a time, the harmonics, building resonance until the blood thundered in her veins and she felt the capillaries begin to yield in throat and mouth, in lips and tongue. Singing, aping the jewel, mastering it.

Killing it.

And killing Marta Caine.

Dumarest saw her stagger as the jewel exploded in her hands. A puff of brilliance which accompanied a sudden, crystalline, shatter. A rain of fragments fell from the opening fingers, the falling hands. A glittering rain which sprayed to a widening shower as the thin body wafted the air in its fall.

"Marta!" Santis was at her side, cradling her sagging head as he expertly checked for signs of life. As Dumarest knelt at his side he said, "She's gone, Earl. Dead."

"Dead?" Kemmer looked stunned. "But how? Who did it? That woman?" He glared at Ellain where she stood, face buried in her arms. "That red-haired bitch? Was she responsible?"

"Steady!" Dumarest reached out and touched the thin face. Glitter stained his fingers as he lifted them from the flaccid skin. "Her heart went or her nerves gave out or something yielded in her brain. How did she get so thin? Wasn't she eating?"

"The jewel, Earl." Santis closed the staring eyes. "It sucked her life."

"Didn't she know? Didn't she care?" Dumarest remembered the casino. "The fool. I tried to help her. There was no need for this."

"Perhaps she'd given up." Gently the mercenary rested her head on the glittering floor. A rasp of his hand and shards of the broken jewel rested against her cheek. "I've been watching her. Half the time she only pretended to eat and when you're old you lose energy fast. She was older than we guessed. And, maybe, she was happy to go."

To die with her jewel: the toy which had graced her life. To end in song and a bright, wonderful, glittering rain. She could have done a lot worse.

Chapter Seven

"Earth?" Alejandro Jwani pursed his lips and frowned. "Was it mentioned?"

"We spoke of it," said Dumarest. "At the party."

"Tariq's affair? I heard about what happened. A damned shame. Tariq got more than he bargained for. I suppose it put an end to the festivities?" Jwani sighed as Dumarest nodded. "To be expected. A pity I missed it but, as you know, I had to leave early."

"You were ill."

"I was drunk." Jwani smiled. "You don't have to be polite with me, Earl. I'm not such a fool as not to know my own failings. Wine is one of them. I have others." He gestured at the room. "The evidence is all about you."

The chamber was long, wide, the roof a semi-circular vault. The walls were hung with maps, diagrams, schematics. Models stood on low stands, some working with a silent efficiency, others immobile. Benches held a litter of tools and apparatus. The roof was studded with lights; some of changing hue and brilliance, others with a baleful glare. A study and workroom into which Dumarest had been shown by an attendant. Jwani had joined him from his own personal quarters beyond a narrow door.

Now, pausing by a table, he said, "I am forgetting to be hospitable. Something to drink? I've wine and spirits and coffee if you prefer something innocuous. Or would you care to join me in a rather excellent tisane?" He beamed as Dumarest nodded. "Good. It will only take a few moments."

It took three minutes during which time Dumarest examined some of the furnishings, turning to accept a steaming cup from his host. It was of delicate porcelain ornamented with sinuous shapes holding orbs in their gaping jaws. The vapor rising from it held the scent of pine. The tisane itself was refreshingly tart.

"That's better!" Jwani helped himself to more. "Drugs have their uses but nothing can beat a good cup of tisane to settle the stomach. Earth, eh? Did we really talk about it?"

"Briefly, yes. Then you went on to discuss semantics and philosophy." Dumarest added, "We also drank a toast."

"To my health." Jwani looked at his tisane. "It seems I needed it. But what about Earth?"

"I heard that you had been there."

"Ridiculous! Did Ellain give you that impression? She can sing like an angel but at times she doesn't seem to listen. I may have spoken about Earth but only as a world I've heard about. I certainly have never been there. Has anyone?"

"I should think so."

"Visit a place which doesn't exist?" Jwani shook his head. "I hardly think it possible. The world is a legend; one among many. I checked after I heard about it and couldn't find it listed in any almanac. That settles it, surely? If it existed it would be listed."

All known worlds were but that meant nothing and a man of Jwani's intelligence must know it. Dumarest said, quietly, "On Harge they claim that nothing can survive a storm. The sannak survive. Obviously they must be an illusion."

"Because, if real, they couldn't survive." Jwani clapped his hands in appreciation. "A syllogism! Earl, you are a man after my own heart. Have you heard the one about the woman?" Smiling he told it. "No woman has three heads. A woman has one head more than no woman. A woman, therefore, has four heads. Ridiculous, isn't it? Yet I won two thousand from Elmay Taiyah on that only a couple of weeks ago. He had to agree my logic was impeccable because he was unable to show me the flaw."

"Did you tell him?"

"Of course not. Could you?"

"The term 'no woman' is being used in a double-sense," said Dumarest. "So, while each of the two premises is correct when regarded apart they can only give a false conclusion when taken as equal." He added, wryly, "But your friend shouldn't feel too bad. While it is true that no woman has four heads many have two faces."

"Brilliant!" Jwani beamed his pleasure. "Earl, you deserve an apology. When Ellain mentioned you I'd expected to meet some traveler with a short temper and a way with women. I was too drunk last night to recognize your talents. Two faces!" The beam turned into a chuckle. "I must tell Elmay that. He will appreciate it and if you knew his wife you'd understand why. If ever a woman had two faces it is she—and both are sour." Sobering, he said, thoughtfully, "I get your point, Earl. The fact that Earth isn't listed is no real proof that it doesn't exist. But it poses a problem if ever you'd want to find it."

One which had come to dominate his life; to find Earth and return to the planet of his birth. He had gathered clues; an alternative name, Terra, the position of the planet in the galaxy; somewhere toward the rim where stars were few and journeys long. And it had a single, silver moon.

He said, "Assuming Earth exists why would it not be listed?"

"Who knows?" Jwani shrugged. "Lost, perhaps? Forgotten? Or if it is a world of legend such as Jackpot or Bonanza then there was nothing to list. But that isn't answering your question. The assumption is that the planet is real but, for some reason, uncharted. Frankly, Earl, I don't know."

A wall, one he had bumped into so many times before, and Dumarest felt again the quenching of hope. But still there could be information to be gained.

"This person from whom you heard the name—did he say more?"

"Vy Wene? No."

"Does he live on Harge?"

"No. He came with a party to buy tranneks and, naturally, came to see me. I hosted him and we had long talks. He also was fond of wine and shared my pleasure in logic games. It was he who told me of the woman with the multiple heads. There were others—so many I've forgotten—but once we got onto the subject of legendary worlds and Earth was mentioned. He said that some believed all humanity had originated on one planet and that world was Earth. They had spread to other systems and settled to grow and move on. And ingenious theory but obviously illogical. How could one world have supported all the diverse races we know? All stemming from one world would surely look and be alike; the same conditions must produce the same shape, form and color. I pointed this out to him and he agreed with the basic idiocy of the belief."

"The Original People," said Dumarest.

"What?"

"Nothing." The man had given no response and it was highly improbable that he was one of them. "Just a sect which holds the beliefs you mentioned. They are very secretive. Did your friend speak of them?"

"No. Vy Wene had other things on his mind. The price of tranneks for one." Jwani smiled at pleasant memories. "Storms had been many, ships few and the price was high. "Earl, I am remiss! Some coffee now, laced with some rare brandy and topped with a rich cream. I have a knack with it."

It was hot, sweet and surprisingly pleasant. Dumarest sipped, watching Jwani as he lifted his face from his cup, lips wreathed with cream. For a moment he resembled a clown, then, as he wiped away the whiteness, he was himself again; a man who masked his inner self and was more cunning than he appeared.

The lie he must have spread about his pre-collapse amnesia—a man, drunk and by his own admission unable to remember, could pick up useful information from those too trusting to guard their tongues. And none but the wealthy could afford to live in the style he enjoyed. Dumarest had no illusions about the rich. To be that way and stay that way they needed to be far from stupid.

He said, "A personal question, Alejandro, you will not take offense?"

"Can any be taken when none is intended? What is it, Earl?"

"I had the impression you were a hunter. But on Harge? And you mentioned selling and—" His hand moved to take in the room. "A hobby?"

"What do you do, Earl? Travel and fight and do what? Look for Earth?" Jwani smiled as Dumarest nodded. "I like a man who is honest and I will respond in kind. I am, in a way, a hunter. Not to kill beasts and collect their heads as trophies but for something else. And, yes, much in this room constitutes a hobby. Look!" He led the way to where a complex machine stood beneath a transparent dome. Within it a disc spun and a lamp winked intermittently from a point at the summit. "Perpetual motion, Earl. Or as near to it as we could ever come. The disc is supported and held by a magnetic field induced in near-absolute temperature. The cold has turned the metal into a super-conductor in which all resistance has been abolished. That is perpetual motion; an impulse received will circulate without loss until heat is applied or the model collapses. Of course a machine built on these principles could only operate on frozen worlds or in space itself."

"The energy output must be small," said Dumarest. "What use would it be?"

"The energy output would be almost negligible," corrected Jwani. "You can't get out what you don't put in. But there is a slight imbalance in our favor; enough for the thing to be useful as a low-power radio beacon or something like that. And this." He moved on. "A set of perfect bearings, Earl. They will last until the steel they support has worn away and still be perfect."

Dumarest leaned forward to look at the ball-race, the odd color of the bearings it contained. "They look like stones."

"They are stones; tranneks. I hunt for them and I sell them." Jwani added after a pause, "I also deal in them."

Dumarest looked closer at the bearings. They held shimmers as of trapped light and their surfaces were polished to the smoothness of oil. Each was about an inch in diameter.

"Tranneks," said Jawani. "I have better ones over here."

They rested in a safe which he opened to display them on a nest of wadding. Black softness which accentuated their shimmering beauty, colors flowing over their surfaces as he moved them beneath the light.

"The hardest things known, Earl. Harder by far than diamond. They make wonderful bearings but to use them so is to waste their potential. They have the ability to take all energy directed against one hemisphere and render it into a coherent beam. You know about lasers? The jewel they contain does the same. But these are far more efficient and far more versatile. They can take any energy; light, sound, vibration, and turn it into a shaft of compact power. They are used a lot in mining and construction; tunneling, bores and the like. The very noise of the drills can be recycled into a cutting beam." He replaced them in the safe. "Naturally they are extremely valuable."

"And you mine them?"

"No, Earl, hunt for them. Here, mostly." He rested his hand on a map hanging beside the safe. "In the Goulten Hills. With a little luck a man could pick up a fortune."

Kemmer said, "No! For God's sake, man, are you out of your mind? If you want to die why not open a vein and have done with it?" He paced the floor to the far wall, turned, paced back again. Five steps—Marta's room was small. "Earl, you're crazy!"

From where he sat on the edge of the narrow bed Santis rumbled, "Slow down, Maurice. No one's twisting your arm. You don't have to join in."

"Have I a choice?" The trader was bitter. "I'm stuck, caught in this damned trap like a fly on glue. If Marta hadn't died—" He looked at the room, the bare walls, the naked floor. The place was like a cell—only the fact that he could open the door and walk out saved it from being a jail. "But to hunt sannaks! Haven't you had enough of them? The one you faced was big enough but outside they grow ten times as large."

"We're not hunting them," explained Dumarest patiently. "We need to find out where they have their lairs. We don't have to kill them or even see them. All we want is to collect their droppings."

Waste and regurgitations contained the cleaned and polished nodules they ate with other stone from desert and mountain; the trannaks which rested in the vicinity and could buy freedom. Santis nodded as, again, Dumarest relayed what he had learned from Jwani.

"I get it, Earl. The sannaks live on crushed and pulverized rock. They need the minerals, I guess. The trannaks must rest in other material which they swallow, use, then void or spew out the residue. And this character deals in them?"

"Hunts, trades, deals, yes."

Kemmer said, "But why us?"

"Does it matter?" Santis was curt. "Earl's won us a chance. Why look a gift in the mouth?"

Dumarest said, "Jwani is wealthy but does not belong to the Cinque. That means he must pay over a part of every transaction to the Families for the use of the land. From what he told me they take first-cut so unless he's lucky he could end by working for nothing. He has to meet all expenses. It would be natural for him to want to get away with undeclared stones but unless he does his own collecting he lays himself open to blackmail. So he hinted, delicately, that if I were to come to him with some stones he wouldn't ask questions."

"Just buy and forget it, eh?" Santis nodded. "That seems fair enough."

"Like hell it is!" Kemmer halted, glaring. "We'd need a license to prospect, right? And how about protective clothing? Weapons? Supplies?"

"All to be paid for." Dumarest looked from one to the other. "It's a chance but it could pay off."

"Or land us in jail for life." The trader was dubious. "They'll search us when we return and what if they catch us cheating? And, if we don't cheat, where's the point? I'm against it. All the way."

"That's your privilege. Carl?"

"I'm with you, Earl. Maurice is talking like a fool. There are ways to hide a few stones. I've smuggled stuff before and got away with it. And, as you say, it's a chance. Maybe the only one we've got."

"You're too old," said Kemmer. "We're both too old. Out there we'd slow Earl down and be a problem. And what the hell do we know about conditions here? I'm a trader not a hunter. You fight men not beasts. Earl—" He broke off, shrugging. "What's the use. As I said before, I've no choice. And I guess one way is as good as another to die. But can we manage it?"

Dumarest said, "How much did Marta leave?"

"This room to the end of the month. A little food. Some clothes. Some trinkets. A little money." Kemmer was bleak. "Nothing else."

"How about her fees?"

"It costs to die on Harge," explained the mercenary. "The bastards charge for collection and disposal."

"There should be compensation," said Kemmer. "That red-haired woman broke the jewel and caused Marta's death. Can't we demand something as damages? Take her to court, maybe?"

"She sang," said Dumarest. "And that's all she did. She sang and the jewel broke. All right, we know she did it by inducing a resonance in the gem and we can guess it was deliberate but how to prove it? And Marta was old and hadn't been taking care of herself—no, we'd run into debt for no purpose."

"How about Jwani?" Santis added. "He hopes to gain so why isn't he willing to help us?"

"He's willing to tell us how to find the stones. Supply maps and other things. If he gives more he'll demand a share of the find. A half—the usual arrangement—in return for a stake. And he doesn't want to be associated with us on an official level." Dumarest paused, thinking. "Marta was wily, she knew the value of money. Are you sure they found all she had?"

Kemmer said, "Holding out on us, you mean?"

"She didn't have to do that." Santis was quick to her defense. "She gave us charity and we were glad to take it. What she earned was hers." He looked at Dumarest. "What's on your mind, Earl?"

"Jewelry—personal adornment." A woman like her would always strive to own gems. Portable wealth and always close in case of need. "You found none?"

"Only trinkets. Cheap baubles."

"Then she could have pawned them. Search for the tickets. If you find them borrow to reclaim the pledges then sell the gems and repay the debt. Something could be left over. And sell her clothes and everything she owned."

The woman was dead and beyond care—the living needed what she could provide.

Ellain smiled at the face on the screen. "Earl! It's been so long! Why haven't you called before?"

It had been little more than a day but he didn't remind her of that. "If I called would I be welcome?"

"Of course! How long? An hour? Two? Darling, please hurry!"

She sang as she hurried to her bath, scenting the water and fussing later over clothes and hair. The maid, saying nothing but noting all, was deft in her help, discreet in accepting her dismissal. Later there would be a mess to tidy, clothes disarranged, the bed to be made, food and wine to clear, smoke to dissipate—she had experienced such things before. But, while the rich paid, they could go to hell in pieces for all she cared.

"Earl!" She had not realized how much she had missed him until he'd called. Then everything had seemed a little brighter, colors more vivid, even the air gaining an added exhilaration. Now, seeing him standing before the opened door, she felt the sharp acceleration of her blood. The sweet pain of a sudden need. "Come in, darling! Come in!"

He followed her to stand watching as she spun in a pirouette. Her gown was of soft, diaphanous material, a floating cloud shot with streaks of vibrant hue. As she came to a halt it settled to screen the curve of hip and thighs.

"You like it, Earl? This is the first time I've worn it. I ordered it especially for you." Her face was child-like in its pleasure. "Tell me you like it."

"It's beautiful—but not as beautiful as the one who wears it."

The right answer and he saw that it pleased her. A woman of impulse and one who obeyed the dictates of her emotion. One who could be cold and hard if ever thwarted in her desires.

She said, "Why did you wait so long to call? Did I mean so little to you?"

"I had things to attend to—and a friend had died."

"That poor woman! Earl, I'm sorry, but did she mean that much?" She added, "You'd only traveled together and she had other friends. Why should you feel responsible for them?"

Because of him they had been dumped. Would Marta have died if they had not? He said, "On a world like this it helps to have those you can trust. Santis saved my life, remember."

"In the arena, of course."

"It also helps to have friends."

"Alejandro? You've seen him? Earl, you didn't say! Will he help?" Her eyes shadowed as he told her the situation. "To collect trannaks? No, Earl! You can't!" Her protest was not enough and she knew it. More quietly she added, "Did he tell you the death-rate among the hunters? The risks they are forced to take? Would you have listened if he had?"

"Tell me."

"Why do you think men ever settled on this world? Why the city is as it is? The trannaks are found close to and in the Goulten Hills. Had the city been set closer the sannaks would have destroyed it in their search for moisture. They eat the mountains. They eat men for the flesh and blood their bodies contain. They—Earl, you can't! You mustn't!"

He held her close as she came into his arms, feeling the soft warmth of her body, the mounds of her breasts as they pressed against his chest. Beneath his hands he felt her tremble quiet, turn into a warmth, a heat which rose with demanding urgency.

"Earl!" Her fingers became claws as they dug against him. "Earl, my darling! Don't make me wait!"

Later, lying on the wide expanse of the bed, her soft nakedness lying beside him in satiated abandon, he said into the mane of her hair, "I hate to ask this, Ellain, but I need money."

"In order to kill yourself?" She guessed the reason. "No."

"A loan." He lifted his head a little. "To be repaid with profit when I return."

"If you return." The bed made small noises as she rose to sit upright on the edge. "Earl, I love you. Don't ask me to help kill you."

"I'm asking you to save my life!" He joined her, sitting close, thighs resting warmly one against the other. "You asked me to help you escape," he reminded. "You introduced me to Alejandro Jwani. Surely you knew what the outcome would be?" Lifting a hand he gently turned her face toward him. The lights were dim, colored glows held in tinted glass, but bright enough for him to see the tears brimming in her eyes. "A chance, Ellain. For you to clear your debt and for me to remain free and buy passage. For us both to escape."

"Together?"

"Together." He held her eyes, meaning what he said. "But first we must get free. For that I need money for equipment and transportation. A stake. Supply it and you'll be a partner with a share in what we find." He gave her time to think, rising to pour them both wine, returning to sit again beside her. "A chance, Ellain—one we have to take."

"Earl, it's too risky."

"Life is full of risk." Smiling, he added, "Don't you want to protect your investment?"

"Earl?"

He saw her frown, the genuine puzzlement as to his meaning written plain on her face and explained, "My treatment. Didn't you pay the hospital?"

"No, darling. How could I? Yunus was with me and, in any case, I couldn't afford the expense." She added, as if in justification, "I'd only just seen you. You meant nothing to me then. Not as you do now." Her hand rose to caress his torso. "You must have an unknown benefactor."

Chapter Eight

The raft was twenty feet long, seven wide, four deep, the body covered with a transparent canopy which swept up and over the occupants and driver. An unnecessary protection; the air was still, no trace of a breeze stirring the sand below, but Dumarest said nothing. The driver, an old man, must know what he was doing.

He leaned back in the long seat. Facing him Kemmer sat, shoulders rounded, face brooding. Santis was at his side. Accustomed to uniform and the weight of accountrements the mercenary was at home in the thick coverall, the helmet and gear which was standard equipment for any venturing far from the city. Through the open face of the helmet he looked ageless, like a bird of prey patiently waiting to sight its quarry before making the strike.

"Calm," said a man lower down the raft. He was one of another party. "Too damned calm for my liking. It was like this last year the time Loffrey got himself flayed. So calm he was fool enough to leave off his suit and climb a crag. Then the wind and—" His hand made an expressive gesture.

"I remember." Another hawked and spat, not looking at the rear of the raft where Dumarest sat. "And Chine? Remember him? We found his helmet after the winds died. His head was still in it. Odd that, when you think about it. No body but his head locked in the helmet like a fruit in a can."

Dumarest had saved money by agreeing to share the raft with others setting out to hunt. Spent it by hiring a guide. Zarl Hine was worn, tough, seamed like dried and ancient leather. One who had spent most of his life in the Goulten Hills. His luck had turned bad and Dumarest had found him hanging around the equipment rooms. He had come cheap because none were willing to take him on.

89

Sitting next to Dumarest he said, "Take no notice. They're trying to scare you. It's always calm before a storm but a storm doesn't always come because it's calm, if you get my meaning. You've got to do more than watch the sand. You need to look at the sky, check the clouds, watch for color. The winds can start high and pick up dust from the Allepcian Mountains. They lie far to the north and grow a mauve lichen on the peaks. If the sky turns mauve start heading for shelter."

The same if it showed green from the level plateau to the south on which crystals of emerald budded to break and turn into dust. Or red from the iron-deposits to the east. Things Dumarest had learned with others but nothing could really take the place of an experienced guide.

Hine said, "You won't regret taking me on, Earl, that I promise. But I can't guarantee a find. If I could I wouldn't have been waiting for a chance. My luck—" He spread his hands. "I guess you know about that."

"I was warned."

"That on each of the last three times I went out I lost companions? That I'm in debt? That where I go storms follow?"

"Is there more?"

"Luck," said Hine. "You have it or you don't. Once I had it and made the mistake of thinking it would last. I knew how to find trannaks and would always be able to find them. Then things started to go wrong. My wife left me. My son fell ill. My daughter wanted to live high. My brother—hell, Earl, you know the story."

"Yes," said Dumarest. "I know it."

"I can't blame Myrna, not really. A wife needs a man at her side and I was always in the hills. And Frank couldn't help falling sick and needing expensive treatment. Lorna wasn't really bad, just young and impatient, and Sakam, my brother—well, you can't let your own go down, can you?" He made an impatient sound. "Why am I telling you all this?"

Dumarest said, "Talking can help and I like to know the kind of man I'm relying on. But why blame your luck for what happened? You were worried, maybe a little careless because of that, taking chances you shouldn't and not spotting what was there to be seen. You made mistakes and blamed yourself and, once your confidence goes, what's left?"

"You think it was that?" Hine sounded relieved. "Just

worry working at me all the time? You know, no one ever suggested that. They all put it down to bad luck and said I had a jinx and turned me into an outcast. I've had to sweat just to keep level and it's getting harder every month." Pausing he said, "Mister, one thing I promise—if there are trannaks to be found then, by God, I'll find them!"

He fell silent as the raft began to drop, the antigrav units humming as the driver manipulated the controls.

Without turning he said, "Phindar! Get your team and gear ready. You're first to go."

"This the right place?" A man at the front of the raft sounded suspicious. "I want to be set down right."

"At the foot of Peak 17. Right?"

"That's about it." The man rose, sealing his helmet, his voice booming from the diaphragm. "Come on, boys, we can't afford to waste time."

The raft settled, the canopy opening, the men jumping out after their packs. Without looking back they trudged toward the foot of the hills, sand pluming from beneath their boots. Dumarest knew that, as soon as the raft was out of sight, they would change direction. Favored spots and entries into the hills were closely guarded secrets.

As they rose from dropping the other team, Hine pointed at the desert. "There! See?"

A ripple ran over the sand. A line which wavered, lengthened as they watched, then abruptly curved to vanish.

"A big one," said the guide. "And close to the surface. One scouting for a mate like as not and all the more dangerous because of it."

"Not a female, then."

"No." Hine looked at Dumarest. "You know as much as most. A female would be looking for a cavern to lay her eggs. They run at times but not as often and usually go much deeper than the males. The bulls run wild when they're in heat or affected in some way and then the entire surface gets covered with trails. When that happens a storm is certain." He glanced at the range passing to one side. "Much farther to go?"

"Worried?"

"No, Earl, but the main finds are made back there." He jerked his head toward the rear. "Closer to the city."

And so all the more searched. Dumarest said nothing as the raft moved on, only speaking when it began to drop.

"Not there! Drop us on the summit!"

"You said to drop you at the foot of Peak 86."

"I've changed my mind. Take us lower down and set us on a flat space close to the upper peaks. There! See? Drop us there!"

"It's your funeral." Shrugging, the driver obeyed. "But if you find anything here I'll eat it. Got all your gear? Right. Be seeing you—maybe."

He hadn't wished them luck as he'd done the others and Hine stared after the retreating raft. "The bastard! Earl, you upset him."

"Too bad." Dumarest stood, waiting. Only when the raft was a tiny mote lancing toward the city did he move. "Right, get the gear. We'll rope together and head down that ledge. I spotted a cave down there and it could lead into others. What do you think, Zarl?"

The guide hesitated, pleased that his opinion should be asked but doubtful as to what his answer should be. He decided to be honest.

"I think we could be wasting our time. The sannaks don't run up into the hills. They burrow deep and feed on outcroppings below the surface. That's why the others asked to be dropped where they did. They walk a way then find a mouth and enter to search. This way—" He broke off, shaking his head. "I don't know, Earl, and that's the truth of it. This is new to me."

And to most as Jwani had explained. Those who searched for trannaks followed a predictable pattern but he had worked out new methods based on the habits of the beasts. Dumarest was basing his actions on what he had learned.

He explained, "If we do what the others are doing we'll have no better chance than they have. Less as only one of us is experienced. This way, if I'm right, we can move fast and cut down the risks. If I'm wrong we can go back to the old way. Now, Zarl, it's up to you."

Only a fool would hire an expert and then ignore his advice. Dumarest had deliberately placed the man in charge and would obey him unless and until he made obvious mistakes or showed too much reluctance.

The guide said, "Right. The first thing we do is to seal up and stay sealed until we tent. Out here a sudden flurry of wind can drive grit into your eyes and before you could get it

out you could be dead. Down under you'll be sending out signals all the time and it's suicide to amplify them."

"Signals?"

"Vibrations." Zarl looked at the mercenary. "Each time
you take a step you send out vibrations. Each time you move
or talk. Old hunters use sign language but we haven't time
for that. And there's body heat and humidity. Even with the
suits tight-sealed some gets through. To stay alive you must
never forget what it is we're up against." He turned, looking
at the desert rolling away from the foot of the range, the sky
resting like a clear bowl of tinted azure above. A mote
showed, falling in a shimmer of blue from its Erhaft Field,
sound echoing as sonic waves signaled its descent. "Hell," he
said. "It's a ship."

There would be a storm, Ellain was sure of it. All after-
noon she had sat at the window looking toward the distant
loom of the Goulten Hills, feeling the constriction of her
stomach as the tension mounted. And yet the day had remained calm, the surface of the desert undisturbed aside
from the thin, whipping lines which broke the surface far
away. Lines which her imagination multiplied with dire fore-
boding.

The hum of the phone caused her heart to pound.

"Yes?" It was Yunus, smiling, smoothly bland. "I thought
you had died," she snapped at the screen. "How long has it
been?"

"Too long, my dear, and I am touched that you have
missed me. But surely you did not lack companionship?" His
smile was the bared snarl of a feline. "Am I to believe that
you have waited patiently for me to call?"

He knew, she could sense it, and cursed the spying maid
and her love of money. She must have informed him of all
that had happened. Well, what of it? He didn't own her and
had only himself to blame for having neglected her. If he had
been at her side would she have found Dumarest so attractive? She knew the answer—always she would sense his appeal.

She said, harshly, feigning anger, "Are you questioning
me?"

"My dear, I am merely calling to ask if you will accommodate me. A small favor I am sure you will not begrudge. I

want you to appear at a dinner I am giving this evening for a very special guest. Later, naturally, we can talk."

A threat? It was like him and she was uneasily aware of how vulnerable she was. More now than before and if he should turn vindictive—

"A guest? One just arrived?"

"Yes, my dear. Cyber Tosya."

He was tall, thin to the point of emaciation, his shaven head giving his face a taut, skull-like appearance. He wore a robe of shimmering scarlet the great seal of the Cyclan glowing on its breast. His sleeves were wide, his hands long-fingered, smooth, the ends rounded, the nails filed to slender points. His eyes were large and held the glow of trained intelligence. His voice was a clear modulation carefully enunciated and eliminate all irritant factors.

Meeting him, Ellain shivered.

There was something inhuman about the man, a cold, hard, inflexible core which she with her woman's intuition both resented and feared. A creature of emotion herself she lacked any empathy with another to whom emotion was an aberration. Tosya could never feel as she did. Never know hate and love and anger and joy. Training and an operation at puberty had divorced reason from glandular influence.

Food, to him, was fuel and a body overburdened with unessential tissue was an inefficient machine. Pain was foreign to him as was desire. His only pleasure lay in intellectual achievement.

Tosya, like all cybers, was a living robot of flesh and blood.

Now he sat in the place of honor at the table and listened to the ebb and flow of conversation. The heaped dishes and various wines left him unmoved as had the entertainment provided. If anything they proved the inadequacy of those who were slaves to emotion. But the conversation held interest; much could be learned from a few idly related facts.

"The reason for my visit?" He gestured with one delicate hand. "Harge has always interested me and when the opportunity arose I was eager to learn certain facts at first hand. Your culture is most intriguing. A rigid capitalistic hierarchy with a few owning all."

"The first came, built, why shouldn't they reap what they have sown?" Old Keith Ambalo was quick to defend the order of things. "The Cinque have a right to rule."

"But for how long?" Jen Tinyah, old, twisted, his eyes like splintered glass peering from a tangle of hair, fired the question as if from a gun. "Cyber, can you tell us that?"

Tosya could but such information was not freely given. He said, "If you are interested in obtaining the services of the Cyclan I am sure the matter can be arranged."

"For money, of course." Romi Barrocca made no effort to hide his sneer. "Always it is for money."

"As it should be!" The slam of Mangit Yagnik's hand on the table echoed from the groined roof and sent glasses shivering. "You sneer, Romi, but how are you different? What do you give away? The price your family demands for water is monstrous!"

"As is yours for power!"

"Gentlemen!" Yunus Ambalo rose, hands lifted for attention. "This altercation is unseemly and an insult to our guest. Cyber Tosya, I appreciate your position and am aware of your difficulty, but, as a favor to us of the Cinque, could you not, in general terms, naturally, give us your opinion as to our culture?"

Smooth, thought Ellain as he sat. As subtle as a serpent and as ready to strike. And yet she knew that in the cyber he had met his match. Tosya could not be flattered, bribed or intimidated. What he did he would do for the Cyclan and for no other reason.

"The culture here is brittle," said Toysa. "An uneasy balance which contains the seeds of its own destruction. This is true of all static societies, of course, but here on Harge you have an artificial environment which will accelerate the decay. Unless steps are taken it will occur in about thirty years." He added, "To be more precise I would need more accurate data than I have available."

Facts from which his trained mind could extrapolate the logical sequence of events. The attribute of every cyber; all could make predictions as to what must occur from any event or course of action.

As a storm of protest rose from those of the Cinque gathered at the table Toysa said, "The obvious is often difficult to recognize, but the problem here is one of simple mathematical extrapolation. You have a ratio of rulers to workers which is veering to a dangerous level. To live in comfortable idleness those not of the Cinque must acquire the debts of those less fortunate and so live off the interest. This system of debt-dependency, however, is virtual suicide for any enclosed community."

Yunus, lifting a hand for silence, said, "Would you care to explain? Credit, surely, is beneficial to trade."

"Normal credit, yes, but your interest rate is far too high. Unless the interest is paid each month the total mounts until the figures become meaningless. True wealth is based on actual production—interest rates create an unreal situation and, when too high, must result in inflation and depreciation of the currency. The danger of high rates is that the debtor loses all hope and becomes resigned to the situation of his inability to pay. The owner of the debt tries to sell it but cannot because there is no hope of regaining the money. Once a man is in debt he cannot borrow and so trade stagnates and workers become listless."

"We have ways of curing that," said Keith Ambalo. "Methods of encouraging them to meet their obligations."

Forced labor and ceremonial eviction if all else failed. Ellain shuddered at the thought of it, again, in imagination, feeling the sand-blast of the storm rip at her skin, her flesh. Remembering the sullen creatures she had once seen on a trip down in the Burrows; workers toiling in the stench and filth, crushed down to a level below that of slaves.

"I am aware of your methods," said Toysa. "But they are inefficient. Already you must be conscious of the soaring cost of basic essentials. Even with free labor food, water and certain standards must be met and when the output per head falls expenses must rise." Something the argument at the table had affirmed as Jen Tinyah's comment had revealed the innate fear of the Cinque. A fear Toysa deliberately exacerbated. "Men are not animals. They can think and reason and it takes little for them to realize how simple it would be to end the system which penalizes them. Listlessness turns into resentment, leaders rise and, once that point is reached, rebellion is inevitable. As I said it will happen here in something like thirty years unless steps are taken to prevent it."

They wanted more but he refused to give it. The seed had been sown and the rest would follow. Anxious, afraid, they would be willing to pay the Cyclan for the services of a cyber. He would solve the immediate problems, demonstrate his value by the correctness of his predictions and make himself indispensable to the rulers of Harge. Desperate to retain power, they would become mere extensions of his will—and yet another world would have fallen beneath the domination of the Cyclan.

Cold came with the night, the sudden, harsh chill of the desert, rime glistening on the cavern mouth as the sun plunged below the horizon. A change at first welcome then one resented as trapped body heat dissipated and the cold drained energy.

"We need shelter," said Zarl Hine. "We need to go deep."

His voice was flat, devoid of accusation, but Dumarest knew what he must be thinking. The original cave had been nothing but a hollow in a wall of rock. Lower they had found others, one which led downward only to narrow into an impassable shaft. Later still they had neared the foot of the range and found a cavern which led back and down the roof crusted with pendulous spines, the floor a litter of fallen rubble. Night had caught them in mid-exploration.

"This could lead down," said Kemmer. "There's a continuation in the rear which slopes to a lower level. I shone a light down it and could see no end. A pebble—"

"You threw down a stone!" The guide was savage. "You damned, stupid fool! Didn't I warn you about making noise?"

"Up here? I thought—"

"Here, down deep, anywhere!" Hine snarled his anger. "For God's sake, man, realize where you are! What you could bring down on us!"

Dumarest said, "Calm down, Zarl. No harm has been done. What happened when you dropped the stone, Maurice?"

"Nothing. It just fell. I didn't hear it land."

A long fall, then, one which could lead to the subterranean caverns Jwani had told him to find. Dumarest followed the trader back into the cave, the beam of his helmet light shining, flashing as it hit reflective motes in the rock. Kneeling, he leaned over the lip of the slope. It ran like a slide for a hundred yards then dropped into blackness. The far side loomed ghostly in the lights, too distant to show clear detail.

"A vent of some kind," said the mercenary from where he stood at the rear. "Maybe it goes all the way up to the summit."

"We need to go down, not up." The guide's voice echoed from his diaphragm. He had mastered his recent anger. "Ropes, Earl?"

Ropes and pitons and lamps flashing as they crawled down the slope to rest on the edge. Dumarest lowered a lamp and saw a ledge far down. The bottom, despite the lamp, was shrouded in darkness.

"A long way down." Kemmer was dubious. "How are we to make it?"

"Simple." Dumarest hauled up the lamp. "We'll aim for that ledge and drop down by rope. "You first, Zarl, then I'll lower the packs and the others will follow. I'll come last." He was working as he spoke, splicing the thin, strong rope into a double line. "Lets go!"

Zarl dropped like a wingless bat, lights gleaming, coming to rest as he dropped to the ledge, waving as he released the rope. The packs followed, then Santis. Kemmer hesitated.

"How do we get back, Earl?"

"Climb if we have to. The rock's soft enough to take steps but I'm hoping we'll find another way out. Come on now, move!"

The rope followed him down as Dumarest twitched it from the holding pitons. Another long drop and they stood at the bottom of the shaft. Grit covered it and dust rose to hang suspended in the air, shimmering in the lights as they moved down toward a peaked opening.

They were still within the mountain range and the guide relaxed as the peaked opening narrowed until they had to push the packs ahead of them and turn sideways in order to pass through. A space which would prevent the passage of any large sannak. He grew tense again as it widened into a vaulted chamber clogged with sand.

"Any openings?" Dumarest swung the beam of his light around. "All of you check for openings."

Zarl found them. The guide, knowing what to look for, waved his lamp in a signal. The mouth of the tunnel at which he stood was fretted, sand fallen inside to destroy the neat circle.

"Old," he said as the others joined him. "The others are more recent but none are fresh." They lay to one side, over-lapping, gaping mouths filled with dancing shadows, becoming invisible as the lights moved away. "There could be others on the far side."

Dumarest examined the walls of the cavern as he went to check. The stone was rasped smooth and bore a faint polish. He moved closer, focusing his lamp, looking up to follow the

WEB OF SAND 99

trace of a shimmering blue mineral. It faded a few feet above where he stood. Other traces, all faint, blocked the extent of the chamber.

"Malabar," said Hine. "Too scarce to attract. They've eaten this place out."

A disappointment but proof of Jwani's theory. Dumarest swung his light to the floor and began to search the fine detritus.

"No." The guide was emphatic. "They don't void where they eat. There'll be no tranneks here."

"Where, then?"

"Out in the runs. Maybe in a lair, certainly in a hatchery, but to find one of those is rare and to live to talk about it rarer still." Hine examined the wall. "Malabar but no chinteny. No elmish, either. This place was eaten out long ago. Those tunnels came from questers—young sannaks on the browse. They like to stay away from the big ones."

Santis said, "A bust. What now, Earl?"

"We camp."

"Here?" Kemmer's face through his helmet was startled. "What if we get visited? Other sannaks could want to have a look around."

"We need to rest," said Dumarest. "And here is as good a place as any. You pair with Zarl, Maurice, and I'll take first watch with Carl. Let's get the tent up."

It was small, inflatable, designed to muffle vibration and retain heat and moisture. Inside it they could strip off the suits, cool down, apply salve to chafed and itching flesh, void wastes, eat and sleep in relative comfort—relative only when compared to remaining cooped up in the confines of the suits. With the tent they had carried cans of water, packs of food, lamps, electronic apparatus and weapons.

Dumarest checked his as Santis busied himself with a sonarscope, crouching, leads plugged into his helmet, ears alert for the telltale vibration which would herald the approach of a sannak. The weapon was a large-calibre rocket projector firing a shell an inch in diameter at a velocity which would penetrate a sannak's hide. The missile was soundless aside from a spiteful hum, the explosion of the warhead, muffled by surrounding tissue would, hopefully, be insufficient to bring down the walls of a tunnel. The magazine held five rounds and Dumarest checked them all.

From where he sat Santis said, "You've been in combat, Earl. A mercenary?"

"Yes."

"I thought so. You can always tell a professional by the way he handles arms. Never to take anything on trust, to check and recheck, to examine each load and to test the action. I've known raw recruits go into firing position with stuck safeties and damaged blocks. They last about as long as those who try to fire unloaded guns. Well, those who survive don't make that mistake." He adjusted a dial on the sonar-scope. "Something—no, it must be the blood in my ears."

"Take a rest." Dumarest knelt beside him. "Check your piece while I take over."

"Check it and hope to God we never have to use it." Santis chuckled. "The prayer of every soldier working for pay."

"A long, quiet war," said Dumarest. "No fighting and regular pay."

"Good food and restful nights." Santis smiled, remembering traditional toasts, hopes rarely fulfilled. "It can be a good life if you've a decent commander. Let me take over now."

He settled as Dumarest rose, stretching, picking up his rocket-rifle before moving softly toward the tent. Only a soft susuration reached his ears as he rested his helmet against the rigidly inflated dome; Kemmer snoring or the guide muttering in a dream of vast riches. Lower down in the cavern he paused to study the drift of sand which half filled the cavern, tunnels gaping like fretted lace where the wall swept in a dully polished curve. The beam of his lantern turned blue as Dumarest triggered the ultraviolet and swept it over the grit before him. Tranneks fluoresced in such light but he saw no answering glow. As Hine had said the area was barren.

The tunnels?

Dumarest approached them, halted as he reached the rim of the nearest. The roof curved a clear two feet above his helmet, it and the sides formed of compacted sand forced into a transient solidity by the pressure of the body of the creature which had made it. A large one; the sannak must have been over thirty feet long with a body swelling almost half as high again as a man.

Stepping forward Dumarest touched the side of the tunnel with a gloved hand. The floor, beneath his lantern, was clean of tranneks but there could be some farther down. He shone the beam of his helmet light down the tube, seeing its gentle curve which masked the lower reaches. It was tempting to walk toward it, to search for the precious stones but he resisted the impulse.

Turning, he again studied the wall, shining his beam higher to where a dark opening gaped, one a little smaller than the tunnel behind him but just as neatly formed. Above showed another, more, small in the dim glow, high, obviously old. The marks of sanneks who had come to feed in years long past, clearing the cavern of its mineral attraction, moving on to fresh deposits.

Thoughtfully Dumarest again looked at the tunnels. The curve he had noticed was to his left, away from the cavern. He took two steps into it then halted, feeling a sudden tension, the old, familiar warning of impending danger. As he backed, the roof ahead, without warning, silently collapsed.

It was almost in slow-motion, sand falling, pluming, filling the air with dust, a mound growing with incredible rapidity to block the tunnel, to surge toward him with a low, rasping whisper as if a thousand sheets of sandpaper were being rubbed together, a thousand files at work on steel.

A sound followed by another, a deep tremulation felt rather than heard. A murmur of rushing water blending with the churn of great stones rubbing one against the other. A grind of blunted drills against adamantine stone. The regular throb and pulse of a rotating mechanism which rose from the floor to penetrate boots and tent and skin and air in an awful announcement of the destruction at hand.

Chapter Nine

"It's gone!" Hine straightened from the sonarscope. Beneath the transparency of his helmet his face was strained, dewed with perspiration. "By God, it was close! What happened?" He scowled as Dumarest explained. "You went into the tunnel?"

"Two or three steps only, and I made no noise. The tunnel just fell in ahead of me as I watched. The sannak?"

"Probably. It often happens when one comes too close. In any case the fall must have covered any noise you made getting clear." Hine listened, adjusted a dial, then released his breath in a sigh. "It's quiet enough now, thank God. You and Carl had better get some sleep."

"Later." Dumarest pointed to the tunnels he had seen in the far wall. "After we get up there."

"You want to climb?"

"Those tunnels must be old but in rock they'll be firm. We'd be more secure in one of them—this cavern must act as a sounding board. I've checked the wall and we can make it with luck."

"Cut steps?"

"No. We'll rig a grapnel and throw it into the lowest tunnel. We climb and repeat." Dumarest gave them no time to object. "Carl, you stand guard. Maurice, Zarl, pack the gear. What have we to use as a grapnel?"

He fashioned it from thin metal rods bent to form a bent cruciform with rope lashed to the central joint. Standing back from the wall he swung it at the dark mouth illuminated by Kemmer's lantern, heard the guide curse as it missed and fell with a rasp to the sand.

"The noise! Careful, Earl!"

Again Dumarest whirled the grapnel to send it flying high and this time accurately. Gently he tugged at the rope, felt it catch then suddenly yield. Ignoring Hine he tried again, this time with success. Keeping the rope taut he climbed, boots hard against the wall, walking as he took the strain with arms and back.

The tunnel, like the wall, held a dull polish, the floor clean of tranneks. Dust rested thick on the curved bottom but the wall remained intact beneath the rasp of his gloved hand. In the blue glow of his lantern he saw it sweep in an upward curve, the wall broken in one place where another tunnel sliced across it. Returning to the mouth he signaled to the others to ascend, stacking the packs and gear well back from the entrance.

As Sartis drew up the rope Dumarest explained, "We don't need to climb higher. This tunnel will take us. We need to find a junction which is both firm and even. A spot giving us clear views and alternative escape routes. If this rock is as riddled as I think it must be we won't have much trouble finding such a place."

"You intend to camp at a junction?" Hine echoed his doubts. "Man, you're asking for trouble. Each noise will be magnified as if we stood in the pipe of an organ."

"But dispersed," said Dumarest. "That's why we need a junction. And if anything comes we've a chance to fight and run." He added, "Trust me, Zarl. It will work."

As Jwani had hinted and Dumarest's own experience certified. Hunters such as Hine worked to a rigid pattern and were too close to the wood to see the trees. They found a mouth and searched single tunnels risking falls at every moment. Risking too being scented by a sannak and being crushed, eaten, buried alive. Fear had blinded them to what Dumarest had recognized.

"When moving, a sannak makes noise," he explained. "It can't avoid it. So the safest time for us to move is when one is passing close. In the rock we are in less danger than in the sand and can get better soundings from the more solid material. We'll camp, search for a feeding-node and when we find one we'll move in."

"Just like that?" Hine was sarcastic. "Earl, how long do you think we'd last?"

"Long enough." Dumarest was curt. "All we want to do is to get in, get what we came for then get out. The longer we hang around the greater risk we run. Now let's arrange a schedule."

Sleeping, eating, resting out of the suits. Standing watch in the eerie dimness of the tunnels and checking the findings of the sonarscope. Dumarest had other, more selective apparatus and he moved far from the camp to squat in stygian darkness, listening to the whispers and rustles and murmurs transmitted through the pierced and riddled stone.

Giants had made those tunnels, long, sinuous shapes gnawing and grinding in an eternal search for food. Mating, breeding, roving wide. The city must rest in a leached out part of the desert; the surrounding area devoid of the essential minerals the sannaks craved. The mountains and beyond would provide but no matter how daring and foolhardy the hunters might be they could only reap a fraction of the desired harvest.

Dumarest thought of the wealth which must lie locked deep beneath the sand. The voiding of thousands of the creatures over uncountable years. Entire mountains perhaps crushed and pulverized in the relentless attrition which had followed natural cataclysm. Forces which had turned a fertile world into a barren ball of arid dust laced with remaining ridges of jagged stone.

A thousand years, maybe less, and even they would be levelled and nothing remain but a restless sea of wind-blown grit. And the sannaks? Would they survive, burrowing deep, deeper, searching out the last vestiges of essential ores?

A whisper suddenly swelled into a scratching. A rustle became a roar. Murmurs became shouts and Dumarest spun dials to cut down the gain as a thunder of noise echoed from the pickups clamped to his ears. It held, continued as he felt the rock tremble beneath him, then the grinding roar began to fade and he was up and running back to the camp.

"Earl!" Kemmer came running toward him. In the blue glow of a lantern his face was ghastly. "Thank God. I thought—"

"Get packed!" The man had been on watch and Dumarest snatched the rocket-rifle from his hands. "Where's Carl? Get him to help. Zarl!" The guide was at the sonarscope. "Did you trace the direction?"

"Earl, the noise—"

" To hell with that! The thing can't sense us over that racket and we can't waste time. Did you check? Give me the figures."

Dumarest sat, comparing them with those he had taken,

setting one against the other and gaining direction, depth and approximate distance. The small sounds he'd plotted from what had to be a feeding-node had come from the east and the sannak had headed in that direction. Other soundings traced the path of the creatures south and away from the ridge. As he'd guessed, the position they were in was barren, the multiple tunnels now serving to amplify distant vibrations.

"Here." His finger touched a position on a map. "About three miles to the east and maybe a quarter down."

"Three miles!" Kemmer sucked in his breath. "So far?"

"If it was nearer they'd be all over us. Zarl?"

"It's about as you say, Earl. A small node, I'd guess, and that could be in our favor. How do we get there? Up and over then down and chance we find an entry?"

"What are the chances?"

"Not good if the node is deep. We'd have to spread out and search for a mouth then take a chance on its remaining firm. That's the usual method."

There was another but he didn't mention it, watching as Dumarest calculated the probabilities. To climb out of the caverns back to the upper ridge, to walk along it, then to descend would take time and expose them to the outside and, if a storm was blowing, render them immobile until it was over. But to press on through the tunnels was to risk getting lost in a maze and, the nearer they approached the node, the more dangerous it would be.

"We'll go through," said Dumarest.

"Through these tunnels!" Kemmer was against it. "Why man, what's the point? It's taking risks for the sake of it. What if we get lost?" A vision of a nightmare of endless walking, starving, dying of thirst, waiting for the moment when destruction would strike. He added, pleadingly, "Let's play it safe."

"Carl?"

"There's no point in going out just to come in again. I'm with you, Earl."

Hinc said, "I'll ride along. You seem to know what you're doing. We can use the node as a guide and it's possible that some of these later tunnels could run straight toward it. How do we operate? Point, porters and rear guard? Right, I'll take the point." He paused as if waiting for argument; then, as none came, said, "We move in an hour."

It was like a dream he'd had when young; a nightmare which had afflicted him when, after his first hunt, he had seen his uncle buried beneath a fall and had wandered for hours in a mesh of tunnels. That had been at the foot of Peak 14 and he had never hunted there since. Hadn't hunted at all for years when financial need had driven him back to the Hills to earn enough to pay off his first debt. Then the second child and another loan and then the illness and the trouble and now the endless moving through tunnels made long before he'd been born.

But safe—Dumarest had been right about that and Hine wondered why he and others had never thought of it for themselves. Habit, he guessed, old ways die hard and when it's a question of land and search and grab and run and think yourself lucky if you manage to stay alive—God grant they be lucky!

He paused as they reached yet another junction and shone his lantern from one opening to another. The dust was a trifle thicker in one but it sloped up and they needed to head down. One had an appearance he didn't trust, the rock had run into veins of impacted sand and it could fall or be blocked farther ahead. The other? Should he lead the way into the other?

Dumarest said, "We'll halt for a while, Zarl. I'll check the readings."

"No. I can manage."

"You can and will but Santis needs a rest and Kemmer's bushed." A lie, but too near the truth for comfort. The trader, burdened with gear, was dragging his feet and Santis couldn't maintain concentration while battling fatigue. As the guide hesitated, Dumarest added, "You've made good time but we could lose everything if you make a mistake. Tent up, now, and rest."

As he obeyed, Dumarest moved to the junction, squatted, set up his apparatus and listened. The blur of noise was louder now and he judged they must have covered two-thirds of the distance to the node. A hard two miles, stretched into seven by turns, rises, blocked tunnels and diversions. Hours of painful progress marked by frozen halts and stealthy movements. Caution dictated by Hine and followed by the others. And twice they had found tranneks.

Dumarest looked at them, glowing in the blue shine of his lamp. Smooth pebbles enriched with fluorescence created by the ultraviolet. Kemmer had found one and Santis the other, both had been buried deep, both exposed by a passing boot. Perhaps, if they roved the tunnels, they would find more but he could not afford to spare the time. And, at best, the harvest would be difficult to reap with the stones buried deep beneath settled dust.

Time and money—to escape he needed both.

He leaned back, switching off the lantern, seeing little flecks dance in his retinas from lingering images. Flecks which formed a pattern and became the fifteen units of the affinity twin. The secret Kalin had given him, one handed to her by Brasque who had stolen it from a secret laboratory of the Cyclan. Her gift which had made him the hunted prey of the organization which dominated worlds.

One which offered incredible power.

With it the intelligence of one could be placed in the body of another so that the subject-host would be ruled and controlled in every sense by the dominant factor. An old man could be given a new, young, virile body. A raddled crone be fresh and attractive and desirable again. New life. New bodies—a bribe none could resist.

And with the intelligence of a cyber ruling their mind and bodies none of power or influence could do other than dance to the tune the Cyclan chose to play.

And he had it, the secret they wanted so badly, the one they would move worlds to obtain.

The basic units they knew—but the sequence in which they had to be assembled they had lost. And to try to test each possible combination would take millennia. Time they wanted to save. Time he could give them.

And, once within their power, he would have no choice. They would take him and probe him and tear his mind apart and when they had done with him he would be eliminated as so much unwanted rubbish.

To save his life he must escape the trap.

And only the node could help him.

They reached it five hours later, inching forward through a narrow fissure, a chimney blown by some age-old venting of volcanic fury to crouch, helmets touching, staring at what lay below. A cavern as vast as the one they had first entered, the walls crusted with masses of crystalline protrusions which glowed with a cold, unwavering, greenish light.

In it the sannaks feasted.

"God!" Kemmer's voice carried a stunned disbelief. "Look at those things!"

"Like worms," whispered Santis. "Giant worms."

But worms had no scales, no rasping, multi-toothed jaws, no eyes which gleamed like prisms beneath transparent protective membranes. And no worm could ever have been as large or as noisy.

"A feeding-node," said Hine. "I've heard of them but this is the first I've seen." His voice dimmed in the rasp of scales passing over scales, of jaws gnawing at the deposits. "Chitney," he said. "And, yes, elmish. See, over there. The dark purple stuff. That's what holds tranneks."

"Let's get them and go," said Kemmer. "Before those things spot us."

"They aren't to be found in a node—I told you that." The guide was impatient. "They don't void where they feed. We'll have to swing round and head out so as to search their runs."

"Go down among them? That's crazy." The trader appealed to Dumarest. "Earl, we can't do that. It's suicide!"

If not exactly that certainly an invitation for a quick and merciless end. Dumarest edged forward and looked over the area below. Sannaks ate to turn and plunge back into the sand; some lying coiled, others resting motionless half in and half out of their runs. In the cold, green light their scales shone with a winking, prismatic splendor.

"The runs," said Hine. "We've got to search their runs."

"Perhaps not."

"Earl?"

"Animals don't usually void at random," explained Dumarest. "Mostly their droppings form a marker to warn others to stay clear of their territory. My guess is that this particular node belongs to a section of the herd. If so they could well have set up void-points to isolate and identify the area."

"So?" Kemmer, no hunter, failed to understand. "What of it?"

"If Earl's right it means there could be heaps of tranneks just waiting to be collected," said the mercenary. "But what about the ones found in the runs?"

"Odd droppings," said Hine. His mind was dazzled with the possibility that Dumarest was correct. "And usually far from the node." His excitement grew as he thought about it. "It's possible! There are stories from the old days about big deposits having been found and, come to think of it, why else was the city founded? They must have harvested more than a few at a time like we do." And, with the passing of the years, the surface deposits had been cleaned, the sannaks driven deeper, the way to make an easy picking forgotten. He sobered as he looked below. "But how to reach it? A fortune could be waiting and we can't get near it."

"There might be a way," said Dumarest. "We'll have to make a diversion."

Back in the cramped confines of the tent he explained his plan. Basically it was simple. They would provide bait to draw the sannaks away from the cavern, run down a selected tunnel, find and collect the tranneks and return before the creatures came back to resume feeding.

Kemmer, sweating, his torso marked with chafes and blood marking a spot rubbed raw by the collar of his suit, said, "What the hell could we use for bait?"

"Water and what food we can spare. Break the cans and let it spill. That and noise should do it."

"Timing?" Santis listened then nodded. "It's damned close but if we work in unison it could be done." He added, grimly, "If the sannaks take the bait."

And if the tranneks could be found before they returned.

Dumarest said, "It's a risk and I know it. I may have more reason than the rest of you to want big money fast so if you want out I'll understand. Carl?"

"Once in jail was enough. I'm in."

"Me too." Hine, eyes bright, rubbed hands together in anticipation. "One big strike and I'll be made for life. My kids'll be proud of me and—I'm in!"

"So how can I stay out?" Kemmer shook his head. "If I live through this I'm going to find a nice, quiet, well-watered world and settle down as far from mountains and sand as I can get." He became practical. "About the bait, Earl. One spot or two? If we can spare the water and food it might be wiser spread out a little. And the noise? How do we arrange that?"

"The run," said Hine. "We've got to pick the right run. One which leads to a void-point. How to decide?" He frowned. "Maybe we can figure it if we study them long enough."

"That'll be your job," said Dumarest. "You know them better than we do, but make sure the tunnel is firm and close.

Maurice, break down the gear and make up emergency survival packs. Carl, you help me to arrange the diversions. Can you build time-fuses from what we have? Good. I'll want four with variable settings and what charges you can make up."

"Now?"

"Now." Speed was essential, both to minimize discovery by the sannaks but equally as important to avoid the others realizing just how slim the chances were. "We move as soon as set."

Waiting was never easy but during the course of his life Santis had learned how to wait. On Clemantis he had waited for three months before firing the twenty-seven shots which had been the sum total of his participation in a small but furious conflict which had divided a nation and had sent him to the hospital with burns on his legs and stomach. Regrafts had later removed the scars as tissue-plants had replaced an eye, a hand, the lower part of his jaw in the years which followed. Decades marked with pain and fury and the inevitable periods of waiting. But never before had the waiting seemed so hard.

The enemy, he thought. The creatures below which could attack at any moment. Would surely attack unless something happened soon. And what chance would he have with only a rocket-rifle as defense?

Below the mercenary, crouched with Hine in a fissure, Dumarest was just as strained. Mentally he counted the passing of seconds, wondering if the fuses had been as accurate as Santis had claimed, if the charges he had set could have been better placed. Wads of wrapped explosives culled from the rocket shells, set in crevasses, placed next to the cans of water and food sacrificed as bait. Now? Now?

A distant rumble as the first charge detonated. A growl as falling debris added to the vibration and, below, pointed snouts lifted, questing for the source of the scent which had attracted them, the odors of food and water which dominated all. Water, that contained in veins or cans, it was all the same.

A second quiver and now the sannaks had moved to the side of the cavern, plunging into the sand, the mouths of tunnels gaping to show their passing. Twice more the ground shook and again Dumarest was mentally counting.

Seconds measured by him as by the others to unite their movements. Time carefully calculated to allow the sannaks to depart, to let the noise of their passage drown their own, the diversion to take full effect.

"Now!" Hine was on his feet and running. "Now!"

Dumarest followed, cursing the guide for his eager impetuosity. Seconds too soon—maybe they would make no difference but his life depended on that possibility.

"Maurice! Carl!" The need for silence was gone for these few, savage moments. "Into position! Fast!"

They were moving even as he shouted, Santis armed, the trader, like Hine, carrying a fabric bag and a lantern. They would search and collect while the mercenary and Dumarest stood watch. A double attack and a double chance of one team at least finding a void-point. Splitting forces was a weakness but, now, it didn't matter. Four could die in a run as easily as two.

"Here!" Hine slowed, trained caution finally taking over. "If my guess is right we'll score down in this run. Walk steady now. Don't keep in step. Don't touch the walls."

Don't talk, don't cough, don't do anything which could bring down the roof. Just keep moving and try to ignore the screaming need for haste. Walk and count each step, each second while the lanterns threw their blue glare on the floor before them. Search and forget the tons of sand which could fall, the creatures which could come driving through the wall or down the tunnel from behind or be waiting in the run ahead.

Hine led, Dumarest following, rifle poised for use in case of need, knowing how useless it really was. Even if the discharge didn't bring down the roof or the impact and the following explosion the writhings of the injured beast surely would. The main value of the weapon was psychological; a prop to bolster courage.

"Slow down," said Dumarest. The guide was loping at almost a run. "Save breath for the return." A warning he had driven into the others. Older, they would be able to travel less fast, less far. "We still have time."

A margin which diminished as the tunnel stretched before them, the floor clean, nothing fluorescing in the blue glow from the lanterns.

"They've got to be here!" panted Hine. "They've got to be!"

A chance taken, his reputation at stake, if he'd drawn a blank his life was ended. He speeded, running now to where the tunnel curved, lifted, dropped to lift again. The dip shone with a scintillant blue fire.

"Earl! They're here! Here!"

"Hurry!" Time was passing and they had come too far. "Grab and run! Move!"

"A fortune!" Dust plumed as Hine dug gloved hands into the heap. "Earl, it's a fortune!"

"Hurry!"

It was talking to the wind. Dazzled, Hine could see only the pile of tranneks, a vision of riches come true. He wanted them all, each and every one, collected, safe inside the sack, the sack safely tied. Not one must be left for later regrets at money lost. The heap must be cleaned, sifted, searched—never would the chance come again.

"Zarl!" Dumarest snarled his anger at the man's stubbornness. "Come on, man! We're running out of time!"

To drag the man from the heap was to invite a struggle, vibrations which would signal their presence if not create a fall. Dumarest dug at his waist, slipped a thin rod from his belt, thrust it into the side of the tunnel and, jerking open his helmet, gripped the end between his teeth.

Bone conduction carried the sound of rumbling growing louder. Of vibration getting too close.

"I'm going!" One hand snatched at the guide's shoulder, jerked, pulled him back and away from the pile. The other slammed the muzzle of the rocket-rifle against the helmet, metal clicking as it touched the transparent plastic. "You hear me! I'm leaving!"

"No! You can't! There are more—"

"They can stay. We've got enough. Now move before I blow your damned head off! Move!"

Dumarest had resealed his helmet but the diaphragm carried his anger and his face his intent. If greed was to kill him then he would be revenged before he died. Hine stared, recognized his danger, shuddered as a shower of sand fell from the roof.

"I'm sorry! I—let's run!"

More sand fell as they raced down the tunnel; thin plumes broadening to showers, into avalanches which heaped grit high behind. Scented, they were prey for the sannak burrowing toward them. The drumbeats of their running feet echoed their position.

"Earl!" Hine staggered, one hand pressed to his side, breath rasping as he fought to inflate his lungs. "Cramp! I can't—"

"Move!" Dumarest reached the guide and thrust with the heel of his free hand. "Move, damn you! Move!"

There was no time to be gentle. Unless the man forced his body to respond he would fall and to fall was to die. Sobbing, bent double, he lurched on. Before them glowed a circle of soft green luminescence; the mouth of the tunnel, the cavern beyond.

A circle suddenly blurred by falling sand.

Dumarest saw it. Saw too the great snout which thrust from the side of the tunnel a short way ahead. As Hine, in the lead, instinctively slowed he reached the man, clamped his free arm around his waist and, with the fury of desperation, lunged forward with all his strength and speed.

A race which he almost lost as the thrusting head narrowed the passage, barely won as he darted past, feeling the rasp of scales on the suit at his back. But won only for a moment—the creature was fast.

It followed in a shower of sand as Dumarest reached the cavern. The head lowered, swung in a vicious arc, a blow which smashed against Hine and sent both men to the floor. Dumarest rolled, half-stunned, stars blurring his vision and the taste of blood strong in his mouth. The rifle lay to one side away from the fallen man and he reached it as the head prodded at the guide. Rising he aimed and fired; a thread of fire reaching from the muzzle to touch the scaled body, to penetrate and explode with a muffled report, to create a gaping wound oozing with green ichor. A hole large enough to take the head of a man but small against the sinuous bulk of the forty-foot beast.

Yet one which hurt.

Dust rose as the sannak writhed over the cavern floor toward its tormentor. Dumarest backed, firing, adding more holes to the first. The magazine fell empty and he searched for more charges to reload. Before him the head lifted, jaws gaping, eye-plates glowing with reflected green light. An emerald which suddenly blazed in vivid fluorescence.

"Earl!" Santis stood close to the fissured rear wall, legs straddled, rifle firm against his shoulder. Beside him Kemmer aimed the blue glow of his lantern at the wounded creature. As it stilled the mercenary called, urgently, "Down, Earl! Down!"

"No!" Santis had the chance of a clean shot but the sannak was no longer alone, Another had burst through the sand and, even as Dumarest shouted, it was joined by a second. "Cover me!"

A chance and he took it. The sannak, hurt, dazzled by the projected ultraviolet, was confused and would be slow to react. Hine, lying where he had fallen, stirred as Dumarest reached him.

"Zarl, can you stand?"

"I don't know." The guide sweated as he tried. His guts burned and it was agony to breathe. "No! No, for God's sake!"

He screamed as he was lifted and thrown over Dumarest's shoulder. Through the helmet he had glimpses of nightmare; menacing shapes, threads of fire, the blossoms of explosions and points of blazing green fire. Above all was the pain—dear God, the pain!

Darkness came as a blessing and he sagged, one hand closing with a grip of steel on the bulging sack slung at his waist.

Chapter Ten

The Cinque had been generous. Tosya had been given an apartment as luxurious as any in the city but the elaborate paintings, the vases, statuettes and all the other items of worth which graced the suite meant as little to him as had the food and wines at the dinner. The only thing he found to admire in the entire complex was the acoustic quality of the main room which revealed an unexpected mathematical precision.

It gave the thin voice of Jen Tinyah a deepened resonance.

"You are satisfied with the accommodation, Cyber Tosya?"

"It will serve."

"We are happy to do our best to accommodate any servant of the Cyclan. I regret the necessity of the ship in which you arrived having had to leave. The captain, well, such men are inclined to be over-anxious."

And, on Harge, with reason. Tosya said, "If you were to build an underground installation suitable for the housing of vessels against the storms, your trade would increase by a factor of at least twelve hundred percent. The installation would, naturally, include a warehouse complex and small processing plants. This, together with a higher rate of tourism, would expand your economy and enhance your stability."

"Stability." Jen Tinyah pulled at his lower lip. "I would like to discuss that matter with you. The question of the social stability of Harge has long been a source of concern to me and to my Family. If there should be a failure to maintain the order of things we would like to ensure our wealth and influence. You understand?"

Too well and Tosya, if he had owned the ability to enjoy humor, would have smiled. The old pattern, both predictable

115

and inevitable. When the foundations began to crumble each looked after his own.

He said, "I will bear it in mind, my lord. But if I am to be of real assistance it is essential that I be given full access to all local data. You are computerized?"

"Not totally. But you can use the phone and I will give instructions to all departments that you are to be given all aid in the name of the Cinque."

An irritation and yet more proof of the inefficient running of the city. A natural result of the Family's mutual suspicion and desire for individual secrecy. Such an outlook blinded them to the obvious—even the merest acolyte could have told them of the worth of a protective installation. Told them too how easily it could be accomplished with the aid of the debtors to provide labor. Some power, some forming mechanisms, the use of a little machinery and the rest done with the muscle and sweat of those who would work to help clear their burdens of mounting interest.

Free labor—but they refused to see it. The common fault of capitalistic societies and the more so when they operated on a basis of wild usury. Interest was not actual money but simply a paper figure. It could be cancelled without real loss And, if replaced by a viable construction, there could only be gain.

Alone Tosya busied himself with the phone.

It was work better done by an acolyte and he regretted the absence of his usual aides, but one had fallen sick and the other, newly promoted, had left to take up a post on a minor world. He would be given others but, in the meantime, he must work alone.

To the face appearing on the screen he said, "Full details of all arrivals on the last three vessels. Names of captains of those vessels, points of departure and intended destinations."

An elementary check which would be followed by others. The city was relatively small, contained, it would be impossible for anyone to hide in it for long—not when the trained and perceptive mind of a cyber could predict where and when he would be.

A simple problem and one hardly worthy of his talents but Tosya knew the importance of his mission. That had been made clear when he had been instructed to order the diversion of the ship in which he was traveling to Harge. An order

emphasized by the authority of the Cyclan and the reward
the captain would receive for obedience.

The phone rang; he answered, listened, gave other instructions. Again, as he waited, he reviewed the situation and felt
a mounting satisfaction. It was impossible for him to fail or,
if not impossible, the probability was so remote as to be
negligible. It would be as well, perhaps, to so inform Central
Intelligence. And yet he hesitated.

The possibility of failure always remained.

Nothing was or could ever be one hundred percent certain.
Always there was the possibility of the unknown factor which
could upset the most carefully calculated prediction. And
Dumarest seemed to have the faculty of attracting such unknown factors. Too often in the past had unforeseen circum-
stances enabled him to escape from the traps which should
have contained him. Too many agents and cybers had died,
paying the penalty of failure even in the moment of imagined
triumph.

No, it was better to wait, to be certain.

And yet the temptation remained—to retire to his couch
and activate the band locked around his wrist which created
a zone of force to baffle any prying electronic eye or ear.
Then to relax and concentrate on the Samatchazi formulae
and to lose all sensory perception so that, locked within the
prison of his skull, his brain ceased to be irritated by external
stimuli. Only then would the grafted Homochon elements become active and rapport be gained.

And, with it, communication with the central intelligence
which rested buried beneath miles of rock which protected
the headquarters of the Cyclan. There would be no verbal
delays; his information would be sucked from his mind as
water was absorbed by a sponge—almost instantaneous trans-
mission against which the speed of light was a crawl.

And, after, would come the thrilling exuberance of mental
stimulation as the Homochon elements sank back into quies-
cence and the machinery of the body began to realign itself
with cerebral control. A brief period in which he would drift
in an enveloping darkness sensing strange concepts and novel
situations—affected by the scraps of overflow from other intelligences, the residue of other communications. Living in
the aura surrounding the tremendous cybernetic complex
which was the heart of the Cyclan.

One day he would join it. His body would age and his senses dull but his mind and ego would be saved. They would take him and remove the brain from his skull and immerse it in a vat of nutrient fluids. Attached to a mechanical life-support system he would remain alive and fully aware. He would combine with those other intelligences housed in the multitude of brains forming the complex and share in their potential immortality.

The reward of every cyber if he did not fail.

Hine was dead. He lay where Dumarest had placed him, one hand still gripping the bag around his waist, his face beneath the transparency puffed, the eyes staring, blood thick around the mouth.

"Crushed." Santis looked up from where he knelt beside the body. "He was dying when you lifted him, Earl. Dead before we reached the fissure." He forced the bag from the dead fingers. "At least you were lucky—we found nothing. A wasted journey."

One not yet over. From where he leaned against the wall Kemmer said, "God, won't they ever stop? The damned things are still after us."

On the scent and getting close. He could still see the thrusting snouts probing the fissure into which they had run. Remember too the fury of activity as they had fought to get beyond reach of the creatures. His bulk jamming in the narrow opening, Dumarest hauling him clear, Santis standing and firing as they gained distance, Dumarest covering their escape in turn.

But, even now, they had no time in which to rest. Through the conducting material of his helmet he could hear the loudening grinding which told of advancing destruction.

"Earl—"

"Wait!" Dumarest was stooped over the dead man. He handed the trader Hine's belt and lantern. The tent together with the radio and other remains of their supplies had been cached in a small junction. "Carl, take a sounding from that crack." He pointed to a spot facing the trader. "Hear anything?"

"Yes—and close."

An attack from two sides, then, and there could be more. Dumarest lay prone, head twisted so as to rest against the floor. The sound almost deafened him.

"Up!" He rose to his feet. "Take the lead, Carl. Head up that crack and take any tunnel you find heading to the right. We've got to recover the tent. Get after him, Maurice. Move!"

Kemmer hesitated, looking at Dumarest where he stood beside the dead man.

"You're not thinking of carrying him with us?"

"No. Now hurry!"

Hine was dead but could still help the living. Odors rose as Dumarest ripped open his helmet and suit; the scent of meat and moisture, of minerals and bone, an attraction to the sannaks pressing close and one which could fetch others lying ahead to join the feast.

One came writhing from a narrow tunnel a few yards beyond where Santis hugged the rock. A small creature which flopped and twisted like a snake to lunge at the body as the floor rose in splintered shards and pluming dust as another grabbed at the prey.

"Hurry!" Dumarest urged the others on as a mass of scaled and furious shapes began to fight over the dead guide. "Quick—before they scent us!"

They would follow but first they would feed and precious time would be won. Time in which they crept down narrow tunnels, wider cracks, plunged into a broad passage, listening, pressing on, following discovered signs with mounting relief.

"Thank God!" Kemmer, sweating in his suit, voiced his worry. "I thought we'd got lost. That we'd never find the tent and radio. That—" He broke off as he followed Santis around a turn. "Hell!"

They had found the cache but a sannak had found it first. The tent was ripped, the supplies it had contained gone, the apparatus a mass of splintered shards. Some had been devoured, none was usable.

In the glow of a lantern a trannek glowed in silent mockery.

"Consolation," said Kemmer bitterly as Dumarest picked it up. "What the hell do we do now?"

"Climb." Dumarest was curt. "We've got to make our way to the summit."

"And then what? How do we summon a raft to pick us up without a radio?"

"Signal." Tired, the mercenary was curt. "Make smoke, a light, anything."

"Use this, perhaps?" The trader looked at his lantern. "Would it carry? The only use I've found for it so far is to dazzle the sannaks with the ultraviolet. It makes their eye plates glow like a trannek. Why didn't Hine tell us that? Maybe he didn't know. That means we could sell the information—" He was babbling and knew it. With an effort he broke off the monotone and said, "We'll think of something. First we have to reach the open air. Which way, Earl?"

A tunnel sloping upward which they left to swarm up a snaking vent, leaving it to crawl along a narrowing ledge which fell away to an echoing chasm. Crouched on the lip Dumarest looked upward, seeing in the beam of his helmet light a jagged fissure. A jump and his gloved hands caught the edge, a heave and he was firm and leaning down to grip Kemmer's wrist, hauling as Santis pushed. A struggle, a moment of heart-stopping, tottering imbalance and he was up, safely past as the mercenary rose to take Dumarest's place.

"Wait!" He sagged, the sound of his breathing loud in the stillness. One hand fumbled at his waist, at the emergency pack each carried. "Your light, Earl. I can't see."

His hands steadied as Dumarest bathed them and the pack with light. The pouch opened to reveal the few items it contained; concentrated food, some stimulating drugs, some pain-killers, salve to ease sores and chafes, capsules of antibiotics. Water was carried in a separate canteen. Santis hesitated as his hand touched his faceplate.

"Open it," said Dumarest. "But be quick." He watched as the mercenary fed himself three green tablets. "Take a sip of water then reseal." He craned his head to where the trader stood wedged in the fissure. "How about you, Maurice? If you need anything take it now."

"I can manage."

"It's your decision." Dumarest glanced down again to where the mercenary rested below. "All right now, Carl?"

"Yes."

"Can you manage to get above me?" If Kemmer should slip, a hand could manage to block his fall and, drugged, Santis had gained a transient strength. "Up now! Good!" Dumarest stared up at the fissure. It narrowed and rock bulged outward from a point high above. Above the overhang the vent could lead up into the open but passing it could pose a problem. Then, in the light, Dumarest saw a thin streak of darkness wending to one side and back to a higher point. A thin crack which could provide handholds and there could be more. "All right, Maurice. Start moving."

He waited as Kemmer inched his way upward, helmet pressed hard to the stone, listening to sounds other than those made by the climbers. Above the rasp of boots and gloves he heard the now-familiar grinding; the churn of crumbling rock, the slither of scaled bodies over stone. Twisting he looked back the way they had come. Nothing. Then, as he triggered the lantern, green patches flared in fluorescent brilliance from a point on the ledge.

A sannak, small, but coming close.

"Earl!" Kemmer yelled in his terror. "Up above! Quick!"

From a point above the overhang more green fluorescence and the shift of a pointed snout. Dust rained from beneath the bulk of the waiting creature.

"Trapped!" Dumarest looked up then down. "One waiting on the ledge and one on the overhang above. We'll have to get the one above."

"Leave this to me." Santis moved then froze. "No good. I can't aim and hold on at the same time. Prop me, Earl."

A chance but the only one they had. Against the sannaks they had only one rifle now and less than a full magazine. Four shots and the creature was masked by stone.

As Dumarest, lifting his free hand to prop the outcurved figure of the mercenary took the strain, he said, "Aim for the overhang itself. Split the rock and send it and the thing down together. Say when you're ready."

A moment while the mercenary settled himself then, "Ready!"

He fired as if he were at a shooting gallery, spacing his shots, aiming each one, sending each into the same line of rock after the other had detonated. Not one above the other but in close juxtaposition so the blasts would augment each other and fracture the stone. As the last missile flared from the muzzle the rain of dust became a shower of splinters, a hail of pebbles then, with a rush, the entire mass together with the beast it had supported.

"Earl!" Caught by the disturbed air Santis tilted, the rifle falling after the writhing sannak, his balance lost and causing him to lose the support beneath him. As he slipped, his boots jerked free from their holds and, suddenly, he was falling.

"Carl!"

Kemmer called from above as Dumarest snatched at the mercenary's belt. A moment then he slammed hard against the rock beneath, swinging like a weight at the end of a line, one which almost dragged Dumarest's arm from its socket, his grip from the fissure.

"Take your weight," he gritted. "Quickly!" Then, as Santis obeyed, "Maurice! Get your canteen. Open and drop it. Fast!"

One sannak was gone but the other remained and could be climbing after them this very moment. A threat removed as the canteen fell to shower water over the ledge and provide a distracting and delaying bait. Even as it landed Dumarest took stimulants from his pack and swallowed them dry. His arms ached, his legs, and his vision was spotted with dancing flecks. The supreme effort he'd made had sapped too deeply at his strength. Coupled with previous exertions it had cost him too much.

"Earl?" Kemmer was anxious. "Can you make it?"

"I'll manage. Get moving now. The next time they attack we'll have nothing with which to stop them." Dumarest forced himself upward. "Keep going until we reach the open."

It was dark when they finally crawled from the Hills. The air held the iron chill of the desert but it was near dawn and the stars looked pale in the cast. They had emerged from a cave low on the slope of a peak and stone towered above them in a series of jagged ridges. A faint breeze played among them, stirring vagrant dust and sending ghost-plumes to dance against the stars but, on the desert itself, all was calm.

"We made it!" Kemmer ripped open his helmet and sucked air into his lungs. Sobering he added, "But without a radio. How do we summon a raft?"

"We don't," said Dumarest.

"We could try smoke, but once we've burned what we have we're as good as dead if they don't see the signal and come for us." Santis sat, head bent, shoulders rounded with fatigue. "Maybe we could contact those other hunters who came out with us."

"How?" Kemmer provided his own answer. "Walk along the ridge until we meet them. On the sand we're asking for trouble this close to the feeding-nodes. Up on the hills we'd be worn out long before we ever got to them. No, I say we wait and, when we see a raft, we signal. Smoke during the day and the lights at night. We could try them now."

"No," said Dumarest. "You're forgetting something. We've hit it rich. We want to stay rich. The other hunters may have different ideas—they'd want a share regardless."

"A big share." Santis was grim. "They'll probably kill us to take it all. And if we signal for a raft they could come instead."

"But if we don't signal or contact the other hunters how the hell are we ever going to get back?" demanded Kemmer. "How?"

"It's simple," said Dumarest. "We walk."

Dell Chuba said, "Ellain, my dear. I am sorry. Truly I am, but what can I do?"

He could enjoy his food the less, she thought savagely. And be more sparing with the wine. And he needn't have invited her to dine with him in this expensive restaurant. Such a place was for pleasant things not the reception of bad news. She still couldn't be sure he wasn't joking.

"Let me get this straight, Dell. You are telling me that all my appointments have been cancelled? *All* of them?"

"Unfortunately, yes."

"Navida Yagnik made a special point of asking me to sing at her reception. Florence Adhalesh advanced me a portion of the fee for me to sing at her daughter's party—how am I to return it? And Matilda—all of them?" It was incredible. "But why, for God's sake? Why?"

"A change in fashion." His eyes were expressionless. "And don't worry about returning any advanced fees—there is no need. As for the rest, well, my dear, these things happen."

On Harge, maybe, but not on more civilized worlds. Certainly not on those with any pretensions to grace and culture. An entire class did not suddenly turn against an artist and for no apparent reason. Unless?

She said, "Dell, be honest with me. Has this been arranged?" The movement of his eyes gave her the answer and, fighting a sudden anger she insisted, "Who? Damn it, man, I've a right to know. Who!"

"I cannot tell you."

"Will not, you mean!"

"Cannot! I am not certain and a guess is likely to have unpleasant repercussions. But, let us say a hint was given, one strong enough for me to accept the inevitable and for me to advise you to do the same. Some more wine?"

She told him what to do with the wine and saw, by his startled expression, he had misjudged her. A lady, yes, but one not wholly as she seemed. One who, somehow, had gained a certain coarseness of thought and expression. At any other time it would have amused her, now she was too worried to feel enjoyment.

"You've been my agent since first I arrived," she reminded him. "You've arranged appointments and fees and seen to payment. You've even guided me a little and held my hand at times when things were bad. But you've been paid for it!"

"So?"

"Just give me the truth. For God's sake, Dell, stop playing games with me. Who is my enemy?"

"Perhaps yourself." His tone was cold and she realized she had hurt him. "I thank you for reminding me that our association was a business one."

"Was?" She felt a sudden panic as he made no answer. "Are you saying that you don't want to handle me any longer? Dell, if I've upset you I apologize, but I'm fighting for my life. Help me! Please help me!" She saw him waver, and with sudden insight said, "Don't give me a name but just drink your wine if you think I could be right. Yunus?"

She sat watching as he left the table, oblivious of the stares of those who wondered at his departure, thinking only of the sip of wine he had taken before he'd left. So that was it. Barred because of a jealous lover—and one who owned her debt. Had he also shut her from the apartment?

The thought spurred her to her feet and out of the restaurant into the wide, glistening passages outside where small vehicles waited for custom. She rapped her address as she slipped into one, leaning back in the open compartment as the driver sent the cab on its way with a hum from its engine.

Yunus?

She knew he could be vicious but how far would he go? Had he bribed Dell Chuba to take her to dinner just to get her out of the way? And to think she had apologized to the agent! Well, once let her get back in demand and she would see that he suffered for this. And Yunus! Somehow she must find a way to compensate herself for his possessive arrogance.

The cab dropped her, the driver reminding her sharply of the need to pay, and she almost ran into the foyer of the sector containing her apartment. Long before she reached her door she knew what she would find.

"Ellain, my dear!" Yunus was smoothly polite. "I regret not having informed you of my intention to visit but I am not wholly to blame. Have you met Captain Hannon of the Guard? You may have seen some of his men on duty outside. Captain, meet Ellain Kiran of whom you may have heard."

He bowed, formal in his courtesy. "A distressing incident, my lady, but one I am sure can be quickly settled. My main concern is the matter of security. If there is a weakness it must be found and eliminated. Your help in the matter would be most appreciated." He saw her expression of bewilderment. "I am sorry. I was not aware that you lack knowledge of the situation. The facts are—"

"I will explain, Captain." Yunus, smiling, turned toward her. "It is a matter of theft. Certain items were offered to a jeweler for sale and he, in good faith, purchased them. Later, however, he grew concerned as to their rightful ownership and having recognized them as having originally been purchased by me communicated his doubts to the Guard. Captain Hannon is working on the possibility of a thief having broken into this sector." He added, dryly, "Perhaps with the aid of an accomplice."

"The maid, naturally, was immediately suspected," said Hannon. "She has been questioned and cleared. All that remains now is—"

"For you to go home," said Ellain, flatly. "Or back to your office. There has been no theft and no breach of security. The articles were not stolen. They belonged to me. I gave them to a friend."

"To dispose of? I understand." The captain nodded then pursed his lips. "Are there witnessess to the transaction? No? A pity. Is the person available for questioning? Not that your word is doubted, of course, but simply as a matter of routine. I am sure you understand."

"Captain Hannon is pointing out that, quite often, a woman will lie to protect her lover," said Yunus. "But I think there is no need to press the point at this time."

"There is a matter of identification," said Hannon. "I would like a complete list of all items given by you to your friend."

"Perhaps later," snapped Yunus before Ellain could speak. "Captain, you have concluded your duties here. If needed again you will be summoned. That will be all."

He was of the Cinque. Hannon bowed and withdrew.

"A dog," said Ellain as the door closed after him. "Too eager to fawn and lick your hand."

"But a dog with teeth," reminded Yunus. "Had I wished, you would now be incarcerated in a cell."

"For what? Giving away my own property?"

He said, blandly, "Certain items are missing from the furnishings of this apartment which, as you must admit, is mine. A small figure of a wrestler made of glazed ceramic set with a profusion of minute gems. A cameo of ebony and alabaster. A vase of elegant workmanship and set with precious metals. A plaque of—" He broke off, smiling at her expression. "Need I continue?"

His own property taken by himself but, if he reported the items stolen, who would believe her innocence?

She said, bleakly, "Wasn't it enough to ruin my career? Must I be accused of theft as well? Just what do you want of me, Yunus? Isn't my debt enough?"

"Your debt! Ellain, my dear, thank you for reminding me. You must have forgotten that you have paid no interest for the past two months. In a few days it will be due again and you know the law on these matters. I would hate to have to take action against you to ensure payment."

"Then sell my debt!"

"To whom? Some young fool like Chole Khalil who would prove his idiocy by canceling it and setting you free? Is that what you'd like?" His face darkened with mounting anger. "No, you bitch! I'll see you rot first! You chose to act the harlot and you'll pay. Dumarest! That scum from the arena! Penniless filth!"

"But a man!" In ruin she found courage. "More of a man than you could ever be. You pampered degenerate! Would you have the guts to fight? To gamble your life? You depraved swine! What—" Her voice rose to a scream as he stepped toward her, one hand lifted to strike. "Hit me, you coward! Hit a woman and prove you are a man! But would you go out and hunt for me? For anyone?"

"Hunt?" The raised hand trembled then lowered as, incredibly, he smiled. "Of course. The gifts you gave Dumarest— not rewards for the pleasure he gave you as I'd thought but a stake. Money to buy equipment." The smile turned into a laugh of genuine amusement. "An amateur! Out in the desert at a time like this! Ellain, my dear, soon you will need to sing a dirge."

For a moment she stared at him then, running to the window, rasped back the cover. The reason for his amusement was obvious. Outside the sky was darkened, the desert hidden by a raging mass of windblown sand.

Chapter Eleven

There had been warning. Dumarest had noticed the changing light, the oddly metallic tinge which painted the horizon with shades of green and umber, limpid blues and smouldering reds. An effect created by rising dust which acted as filters, swirling to change shape and density, mineral contents reflecting and refracting the sunlight. One which held an awesome beauty even as it warned of impending danger.

Panting, Kemmer said, "What the hell's that?"

"Trouble." Santis had also recognized the signs. "A storm's brewing. We might be lucky."

And would be if the storm didn't break. A possibility but Dumarest doubted if it would happen. The best they could hope for was that it wouldn't break too soon. Halting, he turned and looked back at the loom of the peaks now far distant. The marks of their progress lay close behind in a series of small depressions which filled even as he watched. The sand, blasted by arid winds, was too dry and too fine to hold a shape for long. Even the piled dunes left after a storm tended to slip and find a common level, the desert ending in a series of mounded ridges.

"A storm," muttered Kemmer. "That's all we need. No food, no water and near three days walking behind us. God, I'm beat."

He sounded it and acted like it as he plodded with slow deliberation over the sand. Santis was the same as was Dumarest. He had wasted no time starting the journey once they had left the hills knowing that if they had rested, overstrained muscles and sinews would have stiffened. Now they were operating on strength borrowed from drugs, pain numbed from others. But they hadn't dared to strip to use the salves and the rough suits had worn sores in delicate places.

"We'll make it," said Dumarest. "Just keep going."

Keep moving, lifting one foot after the other, plodding on over an endless eternity of empty sand. To ignore the itch and burn of chafed and bleeding skin. The agony of thirst and heat. The taste of salt as a dry tongue licked parched lips. To keep going and not to worry about the possibility of a sannak snaking under the sand after them. Not even to consider the chance of getting lost.

"When we reach the city I'm going to buy the biggest and coldest bath I can get," said Kemmer. "And while I'm soaking I'm going to guzzle iced drinks until I'm ready to burst. After that I'm going to sleep for a month. Then, maybe, I'll be ready to eat." A hundred yards later he said, "What are you going to do, Carl?"

"Much the same."

Another hundred yards. "Earl?"

"I can't think of anything better." Dumarest tilted his head to examine the sky. The dancing shades of changing hue had deepened on the horizon and now, high above, thin streamers of wispiness trailed in faded color. Mauve? Green? It made no difference. No matter from which direction the storm came it would be as bad.

"See something?" Kemmer had turned and seen the tilt of Dumarest's head. "More rafts?"

"No."

"Are you sure?" His voice was wistful. "A raft would save us."

As would the others they had seen since starting the journey. Vehicles apparently searching and from which Dumarest had hidden for reasons he hadn't chosen to explain.

"Earl?" Santis slowed to allow Dumarest to catch up and talk beside him. "How do we handle it?"

"The storm?"

"Yes. Rope up so as to stay in contact? Dig in and wait?"

"Both if we have to. The best thing would be to reach the city before it breaks."

"And then what?" Santis touched the bag at his waist. It held his share of what they had found. "If it's blowing we'll have no chance to strip and hide some of these. We won't even be able to swallow any. Once we crack open a helmet in a storm we'll be missing a face."

"I know." Dumarest again studied the sky. "I've an idea about that."

"I thought you might," said the mercenary, dryly. "I figured there had to be a reason why you wanted to walk. Wanted it enough to make us lie down covered with sand to avoid being spotted by those rafts. Is there anything I should know?"

"Such as?"

"Marta didn't have any jewels in pawn and what we got from selling her stuff wouldn't have paid for the equipment. The money for that came from those things you managed to find. They could have been stolen."

"Would that worry you?"

"Hell, no, Earl! I'm thinking about what could be waiting for us in the city. If they were stolen and if the guards are after you—well, that jail could stand some improvement. There might be a way out. Zarl is dead and could take the blame. The license was in his name. If we all tell the same story and stick to it, use bribery, even, we'll all be in the clear."

Dumarest said, "The things weren't stolen, but thanks for the offer. I just don't want to be skinned at the gate. We've worked too hard for these things just to hand them over. Remember what Zarl said? The first five and half the rest go to the Cinque. That's too big a cut."

He looked at the sky again as, satisfied, the mercenary plodded ahead. The wisps of color were stronger now and little plumes of sand danced about them, lifting to spin to fall and rise again. A sudden gust sent streamers traveling over the desert like smoke from a fire, the same gust blasting a fitful shower of dust against the three men. A gentle breeze compared to what was coming, but strong enough for the dust to scour the tough material of the suits. Dumarest examined his gloves, ran them over the scraped arms, and checked the overlays of his helmet. Three thin, detachable layers covering the main transparency, each of which could be pulled free if too badly scoured to allow vision.

"Run!" Dumarest forged ahead, setting the pace. "Come on, damn you! Run!"

The city lay ahead, he could see glitters from where sunlight reflected off windows, the domed summits of the towers, the swell of the main complex. A hive buried deep, walls the color of sand, only the shape betraying the life within. A shape which blurred even as he forced tired and aching legs into a run.

"Hurry! The storm's about to break!"

He slowed, waiting for the others, running beside them as he attached short lengths of rope to their belts, attaching the loose end to his own. Even over the rising wind he could hear the pant of laboring lungs, the ugly rasp of breath through gaping mouths. Both were too close to exhaustion for safety but, unless they kept up the pace, they were dead.

"Keep running! Move, you idle bastards! Move!"

His voice was a lash to stimulate flagging energies. Santis responded to it, a reaction born of youth when he had trained on a parade ground. Kemmer responded too, from anger or simple fear. Both using the last dregs of their strength, making the last, final effort Dumarest had known was in them. One needed now to carry them over the sand toward the city.

Again it blurred, vanished beneath a pluming cloud, reappearing for a brief moment, then disappearing as the storm broke and the world became a screaming nightmare.

Immediately they were blind. Dumarest saw the outer layer of his transparency become frosted with the countless scratches born of the impact of dust and was too conscious of what could be happening to his suit. One weak spot and it would fray, yield, open to the storm. A stream of tiny bullets would blast in to strip his flesh as driven sand could wear away steel.

"Down!" He shouted but it was useless over the roar of wind. Fumbling he hauled at the rope and felt another figure, the shape of a helmet. He pressed his own to it and yelled again. "Down! Get down!"

He dropped without waiting, feeling the other join him, Santis, he guessed, followed by Kemmer. Beneath him the sand streamed away before the thrust of the wind but he dug, using both hands, making a shallow trench into which he lay. The others did the same, sand heaping on the windward side of their suits, shifting to pile again and giving a small measure of protection.

Fumbling, Dumarest found a helmet and shouted as he made contact. "Carl?"

"That you, Earl?"

"Yes. Get hold of Kemmer. Lock him in. We may not get another chance to talk."

When the storm gained its full strength, the wind, made almost solid by the dust it carried, became a smashing force against which it would be impossible to stand or even lie in one position.

"We've got to reach the city," said Dumarest as Kemmer's helmet joined the others. "Get into the lee if nothing else. With it to block the wind we'll stand a chance."

"For how long?" Kemmer was bitter. "A storm can last for days. We'll be dead of thirst before it's over."

Santis, more practical, said, "Can you find it, Earl?"

"I think so. It's big and, close to it, there could be eddies. They could guide us. Anyway, we've no choice. We find it or we die." He added, "We'll find it. It isn't far."

In the storm anything out of touch was too far. Senses, disturbed by the wind, couldn't be trusted. In the swirling dust orientation was lost and all directions became the same. Blind, deafened, they could only crawl and trust to luck.

Dumarest took the lead. He kept low, equalizing each movement, jerking at the rope when he felt it begin to veer to one side. Santis, doing his best, becoming even more confused but, for lack of anything else, willing to follow. Kemmer, behind him, managed to keep in line.

As he crawled Dumarest counted, measuring distance against time, setting an arbitary speed to his progress and allowing for error. If he'd guessed right they should reach the city before the sand-blast of the storm tore too deeply into their suits. If his calculations were correct they would feel a shift in the direction of the wind as it was affected by the bulk of the complex; eddies which would give them further guidance so as to find the shelter of the leeward side.

If he was wrong they would crawl for the rest of their short lives.

An extra vicious gust and he was rolling, a sharp sensation of heat on one thigh, a burn which eased as he covered the place with a gloved hand. The material had been eroded and had transmitted the heat generated by the friction of the scouring dust. A weak point and there would be others.

Again he moved forward, compensating for the roll, aware of the danger of overdoing it. A small error even when close could be fatal. They could pass the city at arm's length and never know it. And it was instinct to move away from the thrusting, dangerous pressure of the wind.

The next burn came from his back where scales had rasped the suit when running with Hine from the tunnel. Dumarest turned to face the wind, fumbling at his helmet, discovering that two of the overlays of the transparency had been shreded away. If the third went he would have to open his helmet in order to see.

He turned again, trying to protect the helmet, moving on with his body pressed hard against the sand. Another gust hit him followed almost at once by another from a different direction. A conflict of forces which created a sudden vortex; a funnel enclosing a relatively calm area.

"Up!" Dumarest hauled at the rope as he rose to his feet. The funnel could collapse at any time but he wanted to take full advantage of the freak occurrence. "Up! Get on your feet! Run!"

The last overlay fell as he ripped it clear. Ahead now he could see a solid wall, sand drifted high, the shape of domes. The edge of the city and they reached it as, again, the storm closed around them.

"Earl! I can't see!" Santis clawed at his helmet. "The overlays are gone!"

"Feel! Maurice, look for a vent. A shaft of some kind." Dumarest lowered his hands from his helmet, the shielding gloves now worn paperthin. "There has to be some—the city has to breathe."

To breathe and to discharge foul vapors. The underground layers needed air pumped down from the surface and that air needed to be drawn through shafts. Sealed now, perhaps, but seals could be broken.

But where? Where?

The blast of wind eased a little as they crept into the leeward side of the city, swirls and erratic gusts trying to pull them from the shelter, eddies which hammered at them with fists of dust. It was impossible to see, hard to concentrate, but unless they found a shaft they were dead.

"Here!" Kemmer shouted from where he stood against a cylindrical protrusion. "Is this it?"

His words were thin, lost in the storm, carried only by the taut rope linking them together. Dumarest joined him, Santis following, hands extended as he groped. His helmet was totally opaque. Together they searched for signs of an opening; a port or grill, a cap which could be lifted, a scoop to be forced. They found the outline of a flap facing away from the wind, a hinged plate now firm, too tightly fitted to permit fingers to be thrust beneath the overlapped edge.

Stooping, Dumarest ripped at the material covering his

right leg. Eroded by the dust, the suit tore like paper to reveal his boot, the knife carried in it. Snatching out the blade, he drove it under the rim and moved it until it hit the catch. A jerk and the flap was open. Inside was a circular space fifteen feet across meshed with thin struts.

"In!" He guided the mercenary, his own helmet now frosted with scratches. "Keep hold of the struts and move from the opening. Now you!" Kemmer followed, Dumarest coming after, turning to close the flap. The catch was bent and he hammered it tight with the pommel of his knife. "Now down! Move down!"

Down and away from the noise and fury of the storm. Down to where the space narrowed sixty feet down to half its diameter and where a wide ledge gave support on which to rest, to remove the suits, to relax in the knowledge that, incredibly, they were safe.

The jeweler took his time; examining the items with exaggerated care, probing, using a lens to study detail. Watching him Ellain snapped, "For God's sake, man, why take so long? If you know your trade you know their value. What do you offer?" She frowned at the answer. "So little?"

"If you wish to sell I could offer more. As a pledge—" He shrugged, a small, wizened man with old, cynical eyes. More than one attractive woman had come to him on similar errands and some had even returned to redeem their goods. "You will take it? Good. The name?" He paused, frowning. "Yunus Ambalo? Are you sure?"

"I am pledging these things in his name."

"And your own?" He smiled as she told him. "Ellain Kiran the singer? Madam, let me thank you for the pleasure you have given. I heard you at the assembly given by the Guild. That must have been shortly after you arrived. An event to remember."

And praise which warmed her as she left the shop. A small thing, but artists lived on such, and somehow, it had taken some of the sordidness from the transaction. To pawn Yunus's things was a despicable act—but what else when she was so desperate? And it wasn't theft. She could argue that in court if it ever came to it. It was no more than a loan; his goods were safe and could be redeemed. All it would take was money and, if luck was with her, he need never know.

A hope which died as, rounding a corner, she saw him standing, smiling before her.

"I hope you bargained well, my dear." He took the tickets from her pouch, the money. "Why didn't you sell your own possessions?"

She had and he knew it, knew too that the money gained had been lost. And now this. But why had he allowed her to stay in the apartment?

The answer lay in his eyes, the curve of his mouth. A cat teasing a mouse, allowing it the pretense of freedom then to strike, to wound, and finally to kill. God, how he must hate her!

She said, "Either call the Guard, Yunus, or let me go. I have things to arrange."

"The Guard?" He shrugged. "What could I tell them? You pledged some trifles on my behalf. A clever move, my dear, to use my name so openly. Did I give you the idea when I mentioned certain items which could have been stolen? If so you are quick to learn." His voice deepened a little, became a feral purr. "And there is so much for you still to learn. To accept the fact that I am your master, for one. That what I wish you will do. That my command will be your desire. Think of it, Ellain. Our life could become so—interesting."

One in which he would no longer trouble to hide the real side of his nature. He would become the pervert, the degenerate and she would be forced to cater to his every whim. To crawl and kiss his feet, the lash which he would use to beat her, the blood dappling her flesh. She had seen such creatures—despicable toys of the Cinque. Yunus wanted her to emulate them.

He said, "Enough for the present. Let us make a short journey. I have some business to attend to and I'm sure you will find it interesting." He turned to signal a cab. As she entered he said, to the driver, "The Exchange."

"No, Yunus!"

"No?" The lift of his eyebrows was sardonic. "Would you prefer me to summon the Guard? On second thoughts I distinctly remember not having given you permission to pledge those items. In which case, once having removed them from the apartment, you became guilty of theft. Now, my dear, shall we go to the Exchange?"

It was a place of whispering voices as dealers worked at

their trades, relating lies, promises, bright speculations in figures which held blood, despair, broken lives. A large, vaulted chamber, the floor smooth and set with a pattern of interwoven lines of black against the dull ochre. The walls were painted with abstract murals, points of brilliance flashing with reflected light to give the illusion of moving, watching eyes. Benches set in long array and one end was occupied by a dais furnished with chairs and a long table. A busy place with cabs thronging the broad passages outside and with a constant stream of people coming and going.

Some nodded to Yunus while others, too engrossed in business, failed to see him pass. Words hovered about them like a miasma.

". . . for twenty. Initial debt was for five but it climbed. No fault of the debtor—he had an accident and crushed a hand. He's healed now, a good worker and reliable for his wages. Young too. I'll accept nineteen."

And would settle for less. Another voice, this time strained, desperate.

"For God's sake, mister, I only borrowed a couple of thousand! I've repaid ten times that already and now you say I owe as much again. I'm doing my best but how the hell. . . ."

A question repeated from where others stood; couples, small groups, some arguing, others bland, confident of their power. Men who played a game with human lives as counters with no danger to themselves.

". . . old but going cheap. On paper he owes twenty-two thousand but we must be realistic. I'll take seven hundred and fifty. A good investment. You could farm him out and get your money back in a few months. From then on it's all profit."

Unless the man died within a few weeks as was more than likely.

Ellain turned away, disgusted, conscious of the fear which prickled her skin. Here was the place where debts were bought and sold and the final product of the system could be seen. A debtor was a free man. He could not be beaten, flogged, tortured but there were other ways of pursuading him to pay. And one sure way of making those who had neglected their obligations try their best.

She watched as they were led on the dais; the weak, the

stubborn, the lazy. Those who had tried to beat the system by borrowing to gamble and who had lost. Others made victims through no fault of their own.

The tribunal sat and the formalities began.

"Number 49," droned an attendant. "Has refused to meet his obligations for the past four months. Refuses to work as directed. Has been warned several times. No certified physical disability."

The head of the tribunal, an old man, said, "What have you to say in your defense?"

"I had a sickness in the stomach." Number 49 had a surly, disgruntled voice. "It costs to get treatment so I did without. And they wanted me to work down in the Burrows by a reactor. I've heard what it's like down there. So I refused. But I'll pay—I swear it!"

"Unless you meet your next month's obligation you will be liable for eviction if your creditor so desires. The next time you appear before us you will be evicted without further argument or delay. Next!"

A woman with an ailing child who stammered her excuses and promised to do anything to earn the money if only the court would show mercy. The court obliged. A moronic youth who grinned vacuously and was given another chance. A crippled oldster, obviously incapable of heavy labor, who was given none at all. Others.

Too many others.

Watching, Ellain wondered why they were so meek. Why so humble. They were facing personal extinction so what had they to lose?

What had she?

"Look at them, my dear." Yunus whispered at her side, his voice holding a chilling mirth. "Just remember that, if I wish, you could be there among them. Owned interest, the proof of theft, no prospect of an income—need I say more?"

A statement of his position as it was a revealing of her own. She was as trapped as any standing on the dais; caught under a mountain of debt, prevented from working, unable to pay.

And no one would be willing to pay for her. Yunus was of the Cinque and who would risk his displeasure? And who, of his own kind, would work against him?

"The storm," he murmured again. "So old now. Who could possibly live in it? Poor Dumarest." His voice grew hard, ugly. "He certainly has paid dearly for his pleasure—you slut!"

Chapter Twelve

Before them something chittered to run and crouch with watchful, wary eyes. A rodent, adapted to its environment, ready to defend itself if attacked. Dumarest ignored it as did the others. Vermin were to be expected among the sludge and garbage which was the unavoidable by-product of any city. In Harge it was collected in the Burrows; a multi-layered complex of thick walls, galleries, artificial caverns containing lakes of decaying sewage. Of necessity the city had to recycle its waste.

But there was more in the place than the workers busy in the utilities, the rodents watching to snatch what they could find. Among the ramps and corridors, the junctions lit with cold, blue light were patches of darkness and shadowed enigma; narrow passages leading to empty spaces once used now long neglected. Areas made obsolete by the use of new, compact equipment, by-passed in lateral expansion, discovered bubbles which could not be fitted into the general plan. A world where floors and walls were slimed, thick with encrustations, mottled with pale fungi emitting a ghostly luminescence. Water seeped from spongy rock or lay in dew-like condensation on naked stone.

A maze reflecting echoes. One which held the soft pad of cautious feet.

Santis had caught the sound. He said, softly, "I get the impression we're being followed. An ambush?"

Dumarest had also caught the warning signals. He halted, listening, eyes searching the gloom. To one side a patch of fungi glowed a leprous green. Others shone farther down the gallery, dotted up in irregular patches on the walls, some clustered to the roof high above. A narrow, wedge-shaped crack which twisted as it rose but rose only to descend again.

139

"The guards?" Kemmer whispered the suggestion. "Could it be a patrol?"

"No."

"But—"

"One pair of feet," said Santis impatiently. "That's all I've heard. No guard would be patrolling alone and whoever made that noise wasn't wearing boots. Quiet, now, and listen!"

As yet they had avoided the guards and workers, not wanting to be checked or having to answer questions. Gaining time so as to move well away from the foot of the shaft down which they had descended. Time in which to rest and sleep and move on and up through the lower regions of the area. Time in which to realize they were completely lost.

Dumarest looked at a patch of distant fungi. It had flickered as if something had passed before it. The occlusion could have been an optical image, the result of tired eyes, but he didn't think so. Someone or something was out there watching their progress.

To Santis he whispered, "Stay here with Maurice. Pretend you are talking to me. I'm going to see what's up ahead."

He moved forward, boots silent on the stone, stepping like a shadow from one patch of gloom to the next, halting often to merge with the stillness. The murmurs behind him faded as he pressed on, a susuration which lost form and meaning and became merely the sign of living presences. As, before him, he sensed another.

Dumarest froze as, again, he saw the patch of fungi blacken to shine again. A guard? It was barely possible and if so the man could guide them but, if they were searched, the tranneks they carried would be confiscated as undeclared imports and they themselves would be fined or imprisoned. And, if a cyber were waiting, it would be to walk straight into his grasp.

Again he saw the flicker of darkness, closer this time as if, whoever it was had grown impatient and was heading to where the men stood talking. Dumarest waited then followed, dodging the giveaway patches of brightness by stooping beneath them, running on his toes, hands extended, touching, folding to clamp around the figure which suddenly loomed before him.

"Steady!" His knife was against the throat, the edge

pressing in silent warning. "Don't move. We won't hurt you. Just stand still and let's get a look at you."

He felt skin beneath his hands, the warmth of naked flash, a soft, familiar rotundity. As he backed into the glow of massed fungi Santis released his breath with a whistle.

"Who would have guessed it? A girl!"

She was almost naked, the fabric falling from one shoulder and cinctured at the waist covering little more than breasts and loins. Her hair was long, dark, richly shining. Her feet were bare as were her legs and arms. One hand held a scrap of flaked stone and the other was lifted as if in defense or appeal. Her face had a round, child-like quality. She looked about twelve.

She said, "Don't touch me, mister!"

"I won't." Dumarest lowered his knife. "Who are you?" Then, as she made no answer. "Have you been following us?"

"Yes."

"Why?"

"You going to hurt me?" She lowered her own crude weapon as he shook his head. "I was curious. You're lost, aren't you? I can tell. You've wandered too far and crossed your tracks too often to be anything else. You've licked water from the stone and haven't eaten at all for days. You hungry? Want a nice bowl of stew? Something good to eat and a soft bed to go with it."

"And?"

"And what?" She looked at Dumarest with childish innocence. "I'm Ania. That's what the others call me. What do they call you?" She nodded as he told her. "Earl. I like that. Do you want to come with me, Earl?"

"My friends?"

"They can come too. It isn't far. But we must hurry. It isn't safe to hang around here. We'll be safer farther along and in the lower galleries. They'll never catch us there. Come on now, Earl. Hurry!"

She took his hand and dragged. Santis said, dubiously. "It could be a trap."

"A trap?" Kemmer echoed his doubts. "She's just a child."

"Big enough to carry a knife and big enough to use it," said the mercenary. "I've met her kind before; bait to lead the unwary into trouble. There could be others waiting ahead of us."

Dumarest said, to the girl, "Is there anyone ahead?"

"Do you want that food or not?" She sounded impatient. "If you do then let's get on with it. We can't afford to be found here." She added, "Either come on or let me go."

Dumarest had his fingers wrapped around her wrist. He kept them there as he followed the girl. She led them through a narrow passage and into an arching gallery filled with minor trickles, murmurs, tappings. An acoustic freak which caught distant sounds and magnified them. Listening, Dumarest recognized the pulse of machines, the sighing gust of ventilators, a peculiar scraping and scratching.

"It's from the reactor," said the girl when he asked. "They're busy adjusting the ratios. Listen again!" She halted then, as she stepped forward again, asked, "Did you hear it?"

"What?"

"This." She imitated the sound, giving a series of deep grunts followed by a hiss then more grunts. "The sewage farm on level 23," she explained. "They're clearing the processed sludge and making ready for a new intake. Careful now!"

A fissure yawned at their feet. She jumped it, waited for them to follow, then headed into a place filled with thickening gloom. As the walls closed around them Dumarest released her arm and drew his knife.

She said, "You won't need that, Earl."

"I hope not."

"No one will hurt you here."

"No," he said, dryly, "but that isn't to say they won't try. Get off now."

"Leave you? But—"

"Go!" His voice carried a snarl. "Move!"

For a moment she stood there, eyes wide, shining in the dimness then, gulping, she turned and ran.

"Earl—"

"After her!" Dumarest followed his own advice, running quietly down the passage which had swallowed her. If she was leading them into a trap her lone arrival would create consternation and give them the element of surprise. It wasn't needed.

Beyond the mouth of the passage, in a chamber bright with clustered fungi, stood a lone man his hand resting on the girl's shoulder. He wore dark clothing touched with somber hues, the interplay breaking line and form; a crude but effective form of camouflage. He was armed with a spear tipped with vicious barbs and a thin knife of bright steel.

He said, Welcome, strangers, and have no fear. My name is Lowbar.

Beneath his hand the girl faced them, smiling.

There was something furtive about the man, a sly movement of the eyes, a wariness to be expected in someone who lived with fear. And there was a tension in the way he hefted the spear, the manner in which he placed his booted feet as he led the way to a cave. The warm glow of a fire dulled the cold radiance of fungi and a clutter of bedding, bowls, small items made it more of a home than a mere hollow gouged in a wall of stone.

And there was food.

It was what Dumarest had expected; a stew containing scraps of unidentifiable meat, vegetables, a sludge-like thickening. Rats, he guessed, and some of the fungi together with the residue of yeast vats and algae tanks and anything else which could be scavenged. He cleaned the bowl and nodded his thanks when offered another. Food was food and he was too hungry to be squeamish.

"You came at a good time," said Lowbar. They sat alone, the girl had vanished on business of her own and Kemmer and Santis lay asleep on heaped bedding. "A worker was careless at one of the utilities and failed to close a valve securely. The sludge attracted rodents. Need I say more?"

Dumarest threw aside a cleaned bone. "Is the girl your daughter?"

"Ania? No. Only by adoption. Her mother Ran when she was little more than a baby. I found her wandering, almost dead from starvation and other things. She died but the child survived and has been with us ever since."

"Us?" Dumarest had only seen the two of them. "There are more?"

"Many more." Lowbar had shrewd eyes. "But you knew that. How?"

"You have a fire burning but it is too big for just the two of you. As is this cave. And you have too much bedding, too many bowls—a dozen?"

Lowbar nodded, lying; there had to be at least double that number but Dumarest knew better than to press the matter. A guest should always defer to the whims of his host. He and the others had been made welcome, given water, food, the assurance they could sleep without fear. An offer Dumarest had accepted with reservations. They would continue as they had since leaving the shaft and he had taken the first watch.

Lowbar said, "Ania is clever and one of the best trackers we have. She has been following you for a long time now. Only when she reported to me that you seemed genuine did I inform her that you would be welcome here. Of course it is possible that she has made a mistake."

"All things are possible," admitted Dumarest. "But if we weren't genuine would we have come unarmed? Without supplies? Without a radio to maintain contact with others? And would we have been at pains to avoid the guards?"

"No," admitted Lowbar. "And the facts tell in your favor. You appeared lost."

"We were lost." Dumarest added, "We still are."

"It often happens. When a person is on the Run they usually get confused. In such a case they are more than willing to side with those who offer their help."

"You, for example?" As Lowbar made no comment Dumarest continued, "Did you get help when you needed it?"

"I didn't need it. I knew enough to make out for myself." Lowbar paused, thinking. A pot stood beside the fire and he dipped a bowl into it, handed it to Dumarest and helped himself to another. The liquid was warm, thick, alive with fermenting yeast and strongly alcoholic. "It must be twenty years ago now. I'd got into debt and the sum had climbed. No fault of my own but you know how it is. They sent me to work at the reactors. My last chance; if I refused or slacked the tribunal would order my eviction."

"Your execution?"

"Eviction," corrected Lowbar. "There is no death penalty on Harge. If evicted it is theoretically possible to survive. No one ever has but the possibility remains. A fine point but it soothes the conscience of those tender in such matters." He added, bitterly, "It would be more merciful to kill and have done with it."

Dumarest agreed. "And?"

"I Ran. I'd scouted a little first and learned what I could from others. Some of the workers are sympathetic and will help a little, if it doesn't cost them anything. A form of insurance, I suppose, they like to think they have somewhere to run if things get too bad. Anyway, I had some idea of where to go and what to do. I'd cached what supplies I could and when I left I took all I could carry. I was lucky. Other's weren't. Ania's mother, for example. She was caught by a hunting party looking for a little sport and shot twice before managing to get away. That's how they treat you once you've Run. They no longer regard you as human."

"Shot? With lasers?"

"No. They aren't allowed down here. If we managed to get arms like that the Guard wouldn't be able to touch us. The hunting parties use spears and crossbows—you saw one of their spears. I was carrying it when you arrived. Ania's mother had been hit with bolts in the kidney and lung. She died in my arms. I never even learned her name but the girl takes after her in looks." He paused then, as Dumarest remained silent, said, "And you?"

"On the run too," said Dumarest. "And we ran straight into trouble. Can you guide us back to the upper levels?"

"Back?" Lowbar frowned, not understanding. "You want to go back?"

"That's right."

"But I thought you would join us. Become part of my number."

"We ran from the prospect of getting into debt," explained Dumarest. "And we ran into a storm. We managed to get back into the city through a ventilation shaft—a trick others could try." He was being honest; Lowbar had too many men within call for it to be wise for him to do anything else. And, aside from his group, there could be others. "We wandered until Ania found us."

"A storm?" Lowbar was incredulous. "Man, nothing can live in a storm!"

"We survived and so could others. We had luck and some help and we beat the system in our way as you did in yours."

"Help?"

"Help." Dumarest didn't go into detail, if the man thought they had powerful allies it would do no harm. "But we have a lot in common. Did you wait to be evicted? Did you just give up? Would you be sitting here now if you had? You survived as we did and that's reason enough to help each other. We need to be guided to the upper levels. And you? What do you need? If you had lasers—"

Lowbar snapped at the bait. "We could laugh at the guards," he said excitedly. "At the bastards who come down to hunt us as if we were vermin. At the workers who hate us because they haven't the guts to join us. Can you get me lasers?"

"I'll do my best." Dumarest met the man's eyes. It would be useless to promise more and yet, so far, he'd promised him nothing. "Will you help us?"

"Let's talk about the lasers. How many can you get?"

"It depends on the price. And it depends on what's in it for me. Let me think about it. I'll do what I can, that I promise, but don't press too hard. When can you guide us?"

"Tomorrow," said Lowbar after a moment. "After you've rested. "I'll have someone guide you tomorrow."

The storm was over and for two days now rafts had scoured the desert and the Goulten Hills. A vain search, as yet there had been no trace of what he desperately needed to find and, lacking concrete evidence, Tosya was driven back on the cold logic of the situation. One emphasized by Yunus Ambalo as he stood with the cyber in the apartment loaned to him by the Cinque.

"There is no hope," he repeated. "No one could possibly have lived through that storm."

"The Goulten Hills?"

"Rafts searched before the storm broke and again after it subsided and each time with the same result. Nothing. If a party had sheltered within the range they must have left it when the storm ended."

"Must?"

"No water," said Yunus tiredly. "No food."

"A man in good condition can live without food for a month and still maintain his efficiency," reminded the cyber. "And Dumarest is accustomed to traveling Low."

"Maybe, but a man needs his strength on the desert. And what about water?"

"The party carried water."

"The search team discovered the ruin of their tent together with the survival radio and supplies." The cost of the search using highly expensive electronic equipment to track down the permanently active components was something yet to be argued about. "That was prior to the storm breaking. Nothing living was spotted on the desert. The assumption must be the party, if still alive, was within the range. They were not discovered. Therefore they must either have been destroyed by the sannaks or lost in some tunnel. The storm would have trapped them and, if the tunnel had collapsed—" Yunus broke off, shrugging. To him the matter was crystal clear and he couldn't see why Tosya was so insistent. "Nothing could have survived the storm," he said again. "You have seen the attrition of suits exposed to the wind. They could never have made it from the hills to the city. They could never have lasted with the little water they must have had. They must all be dead."

The end!

Tosya closed his eyes and thought of it and came as close as he could ever come to the feeling of despair. To have failed and to be faced with the need for paying the penalty of failure.

And yet where had he gone wrong?

Dumarest had been alive and in the city that he knew for certain. Had he remained in the city he would have been safely held. Even now there was no hard evidence that he had left the confines of Harge but Tosya knew better. The party which had not followed the usual procedure must have had him as one of its number even though the license had been in the name of a resident. All others had been accounted for. Of those who had been dumped by Frome from the *Urusha* two were at hand, one was dead, the others including Dumarest had, apparently, vanished.

Where else but on the desert?

"Cyber Tosya." Yunus made an effort to control his impatience. "The ship which landed this morning will leave before dark. If you intend to travel on it I would advise no further delay."

There was time, not much, but still enough for him to again review the facts of recent events. Dumarest, so close and now so far. Dead, lost beneath the sand, every grain of his body separated and mixed with older, more arid dust. The valuable information contained in his mind lost for what could be millennia.

And he had allowed it to happen.

And yet, could he wholly be at fault? Dumarest must have left the city before he had even landed—would the central intelligence take that into consideration? The one at fault must surly be Frome who had failed to carry out his orders or, more probable, the one to whom he had passed them had been lax.

Was it worth staying?

Again Tosya equated the probabilities and came up with the same bleak answer. If Dumarest had been caught by the storm he would now be dead—the probability was as high as any he had made. He had not entered the city while the storm had been in progress, the guards at the gate were positive as to that. Nothing unusual had been reported and every known fact led to the same conclusion. Dumarest was dead.

Yunus said, "The ship, Tosya. If you intend leaving you must go now."

To report. To serve the rest of his life in minor capacities, never again to be trusted with matters of great importance, never, even, to gain the coveted reward. Yet if he had failed there was no need to compound his failure.

Yunus blinked as the puff of gas assailed his nostrils. A moment then the incident was forgotten—but he was now a man as good as dead. Within a few hours the parasite carried in the vapor would have rooted itself in his brain, there to grow, to distort his cerebral process, to kill as surely as a bullet.

And any curiosity he may have felt about the Cyclan's interest in Dumarest would have died with him.

Chapter Thirteen

The guide was a young man, furtive, taciturn. Santis frowned as, for the third time, he failed to answer. To Dumarest he said, "Why didn't Lowbar let us have the girl? And why keep us waiting so long? I don't like it, Earl. And I don't trust the man he gave us."

Neither did Dumarest. Twice now he had spotted a familiar patch of fungus, the second time he had marked it and now, seeing it again, decided that deceptive tactics had gone too far.

Calling a halt, he said, "All right, that's enough. We'll make our own way."

"You can't!" The guide came back to rejoin them. "You won't be able to find the way."

"And we won't be walking in circles." Dumarest looked at the man, his face hard. "Do you think we're fools not to know what you're doing? Who put you up to it? Lowbar? Doesn't he trust us?"

"You lied. You said you'd lived through a storm. No one can do that."

"So you think we must be spies." The logic made sense. "So you're leading us around to what? A trap? Isn't it ready yet? Or do you just want to confuse us?" Dumarest frowned as he gained no answer. Reaching out he gripped the man by the hair, the knife flashing as he lifted it to rest the needle point against the taut windpipe. "Now listen. You guide us correctly or I'll see to it you never guide anyone again. And if your friends are waiting lead us away from them because if you don't—" The pressure of the blade completed the sentence. "Now let's get moving!"

Shivering, the guide obeyed, leading them up a narrow ramp, through a fissure, along a ledge circling a vent from which foul odors gusted, into a labyrinth of passages, each looking like the other. A maze which confused all sense of direction. Dumarest tightened his grip.

"No tricks, now," he warned. "If anything happens you'll be the first to go."

"Nothing will—we've passed them, all you need to do is to keep going straight to the junction then—" He gasped as sound echoed from ahead. "The guards! Let me go! The guards!"

"No," said Kemmer. "Not guards! They've no uniforms. They must be workers."

They came from a narrow passage as the guide, with a desperate jerk, ripped himself free and raced into the maskings shadows. All were wearing thick coveralls and were armed with long clubs and carrying lanterns. Their leader halted as he saw the three men, club poised, lantern raised to bathe them in its light.

"Who the hell are you?"

"Three fools who got themselves lost." Dumarest threw aside the swath of hair and lifted empty hands, smiling, obviously pleased at the encounter. "We had a guide but he ran off when he heard you."

"A guide?"

"A young man who offered to lead us. We seem to have been walking for hours and getting nowhere. I guess he didn't know the way as well as he claimed."

"And he ran off? Which way?" The leader had a hard, craggy face, It grew ugly as he listened. "Harry! Sheel! Take men and go after him." He scowled as they ran off. "They won't find anything but it's worth the try. Keeps the scum wary if nothing else. You were lucky. He'd have led you into a trap if we hadn't happened along. You'd have been killed, stripped and eaten."

"Eaten?"

"That's right." The man glanced at Kemmer. The trader looked as if he wanted to vomit. "It's happened before which is why we always move around in groups. Lost, you say?"

"That's right." Dumarest shrugged. "We came down with a party but got separated somehow and have been wandering ever since."

"You come down after welchers?" The craggy man seemed to think he had the answer. "It's long past time they were exterminated. They come down here on the run or maybe they've been ordered to work in an installation and won't take the discipline. They lurk and steal anything that's going, attack anyone weaker than themselves and destroy what they can't use. Vermin!" His hand tightened on the club. "Filth!"

"You don't like them," said Kemmer.

"I hate their guts. I've never borrowed anything in my life and never owed a minim. I work hard and live within my means and don't try to get rich quick or crave luxuries I can't afford. If a man's too weak to control his greed then he has no right to whine at the consequences. No one forced them to borrow. They knew the rate. They knew what would happen if they didn't pay. I tell you, mister, the quicker they get rid of the scum the better off we'll all be. Parasites like that are useless to everyone."

Dumarest said, "Get rid of them? How do you suggest it should be done? The Cinque would like to know."

"You from the Cinque?" The man frowned, suspicious. "I thought you said you came with a party."

"We did. One sent by the Cinque. Yunus Ambalo, Jhol Barrocca, Elmay Tinyah—but you know those interested in the problem. They are as concerned as you are. You seem to be a man of firm ideas and I'd like to mention you in my report. If a program is devised we'll need to find a strong man to put in charge. Would you be willing to accept the responsibility? There'll be adequate compensation, of course." Dumarest smiled as the man nodded. "Good. You've an office? I'd like to take your name and maybe we could talk a little. You have a phone? Better still. And, naturally, you can guide us after I make a few calls. I want to let the others know we're safe. Yunus would be amused but others are a little more serious and aware of the problems you people have to face. They would have eaten us, you say?"

He nodded at the affirmation, keeping the man talking, giving him no time to think as they made their way toward the installation, the office, the phone it contained.

Alejandro Jwani said, "Coffee, Earl? Wine? Tisane? Or would you prefer something stronger? We have reason to celebrate!"

"Coffee."

"One of my specials?" Jwani busied himself at the table with his pots and bottles. "You know, Earl, even now I find it incredible that you are still alive. The ventilation shaft, of course. Once we have the facts the answer becomes obvious. I should have guessed when the technician made his report."

"Report?" Dumarest met his eyes as he took the proffered cup. "Was one made?"

"To me, yes. A routine statement that there had been trouble with the catch of shaft 62. It seems that it had been bent then hammered back into place. The technician owed me a small favor and came to me before handing the report to the cyber." Jwani sipped then added, casually, "I suppose I should have passed on the information but, somehow, it slipped my mind. Then Tosya left and it was too late."

Dumarest looked at his cup and saw the rainbows shimmering on the oily cream. He drank to still the betrayal of his agitation. A cyber had come as he'd expected and had left—why?

"The reason for his visit is something of a mystery," said Jwani. He almost seemed to be reading Dumarest's thoughts. "He consulted with the Cinque and made some promises but the only one who was really close to him is now dead. Yunus Ambalo—a distressing case. An infection of the brain which struck him down without warning. At first murder was suspected and Ellain was questioned but an autopsy cleared her. My own conclusion is that he was searching for someone and left when it became obvious he could no longer be found." He drank then, frowning, said, "Is the coffee not to your liking, Earl?"

"It is delicious." Dumarest drank and held out the empty cup. "Could I have more?"

He moved about the room as Jwani obliged, looking at the maps, the models with their spinning wheels, the smooth bearings which cost so much to find. Yet the finding of them had saved his life.

They had broken the web of sand in which he had been trapped.

How much did Jwani know?

Dumarest studied him as he stood at the table. A seeming dilettante but that was a facade. As was his claim to drunkenness and loss of memory. The workroom betrayed him—no man with such weaknesses could have constructed such items of mechanical delicacy. And he had witheld information from the cyber. Had Tosya received it, he would have known what had happened. The Burrows would have been sealed, searched and he would have been taken. A single clue would have given the cyber all the information he needed.

And Jwani had withheld it.

Why?

He had traveled and had mentioned Earth. An accident or a deliberate stimulus so as to study the reaction? Was he, despite his denial, somehow connected with the Original People? Did he work to provide low-energy machines in order to maintain isolated colonies?

Possibilities which must remain mere speculations. It was enough that, for reasons of his own, he had done what he had.

"Alejandro Jwani," said Dumarest. "I thank you."

"And I you, Earl." Jwani's cup lifted in a toast. A casual gesture but his eyes told that he knew what Dumarest had meant. "You have gained a fortune in which I shall share. The largest find ever made. I shall have to dispose of the tranneks with care to avoid the necessity of having to answer awkward questions, but that is a matter of detail. They are within the city and one stone looks much like another."

Dumarest said, "The money?"

"Is yours. You have no need to wait. I've done as you requested; money for Hine's family, Ellain's debt purchased from Yunus's heir—she owed a high sum, Earl."

"She staked us. She earned it." As had Jwani. "One thing—was a clearance found among Yunus's papers from the hospital? One for recent payment?"

"Yes. You expected it?"

"I thought it might be found." Dumarest finished his coffee. "Does Ellain know she is free?"

"She had to be told, Earl. The cancellation of her debt needed to be witnessed." Jwani added, with a smile, "She is waiting for you."

Dumarest heard the song as he approached the door; a thin, rippling melody of dancing notes and unashamed gaiety. It ceased as he pressed the chime then the door opened and she was facing him.

"Earl! When Alejandro told me—Earl!"

He felt the impact of her body, the locking pressure of her arms, the soft, warm, demanding pressure of her lips as they found his own. A moment in which time halted and the uni-

verse shrank to the place where they stood. One which held
all joy, all culmination, all happiness.

"My darling!" She stepped back and allowed him to enter
the apartment, slamming the door shut after him, moving
over the carpet like a young and nubile girl. "Earl, my darling! My love!"

She had bathed and was scented; a perfumed and eager
participant in an ancient rite, but for now it was enough to
embrace him, to feel his masculine hardness, his strength, to
know that he was with her and not dead as she had feared.

He had saved her and that should have been enough but,
being a woman, she was curious.

"How, Earl? How did you manage to survive?"

"Luck."

"Luck?" She turned and crossed to the window and cleared
the pane. It was night, the scene one of animated beauty,
long lines of mounded dunes running across the desert now
streaming as if on fire, fretted summits yielding to adopt new
configurations, the whole silvered by the glow of stars. A low
wind, the herald of another storm, one which would break
before dawn. Until then the dust would stay low to drift like
glittering snow over the rippled plain. "It takes more than
luck to live in a storm, Earl."

She was hurt and he knew it, stung by what she thought to
be his reluctance to take her into his confidence. And yet
what more could he tell? Luck had saved him from the storm
as it had saved him from the trap laid by the Cyclan. Luck
which had enabled him to break free of planned intent.
Luck—how long would it last?

"Earl?"

"I had help," he said. "Without it I would have been lost."

The truth but not in the way she took it. "The guide," she
said. "That poor man. And your other companions. What are
they going to do now, my darling?"

"Kemmer may stay. He's an entrepreneur and, with
money, can see a way to use the system to his advantage.
Santis will remain with him for a while—both need medical
attention." The mercenary more than the trader; old, he had
strained himself to the limit and beyond.

"And you, Earl?"

"I'm here, Ellain. With you."

The answer she had wanted to hear and she smiled her
pleasure as she crossed the room to pour them both wine.

"Remember when you first visited me, darling? How cautious you were? Did you really think I might want to poison you?"

"Such things have been known." He added dryly, "As Yunus should know."

"You think I killed him?"

"No."

"At first the Guard thought I had. I wanted to but I lacked the courage. When it happened it was horrible. I was with him and, suddenly, he groaned and fell. He was dead when I tried to lift him."

Killed by the cyber because he had failed—Dumarest was certain of it. Yunus had paid for his hospital treatment and it was easy to guess why. He must have been acting on orders relayed by Frome or some earlier communication but he had been careless. Besotted with Ellain he had failed to safeguard his charge and for that, together with other reasons, he had been disposed of.

Luck again—if he had kept his mind on the job, if Tosya had arrived before the *Urusha*—such little things to alter the direction of a life.

"Earl?" She mistook his introspection. "Are you jealous?"

"Of Yunus? Should I be?"

"It would be nice if you were."

"It would be nice if we could all be born again," he said. "To know all that we know now so as never to make the same mistakes. How can I be jealous of things which happened before I met you?"

"And since?" Her eyes held his own. "Do you blame me?"

"For doing what you had to do?" His shrug was impatient. "The past is dead—forget it. Only the present is important."

"And the future?"

"That has yet to come. It may never come. All we can be sure of is the present moment."

The fact that he was free and safe and able to travel as he wished. The fact that he was alive. That he was with a woman with hair a scarlet glory and eyes of limpid emerald. One with the voice of an angel and a body made for passion. One with her own fears.

"A ship may land after the storm," whispered Ellain. "Within a day or a week. When it leaves?"

"I'll be on it."

"And me?"

She might be on it too, traveling with him, loving him, wanting him as now he wanted her. But not for long. A journey, maybe two, and her art would draw her as his quest drew him. They would drift apart, she to the stage and he to other worlds. Moving, always moving in his endless search for the planet of his birth. But, for now, they had each other.

And, for now, that was enough.

Recommended for Star Warriors!

The Dorsai Novels of Gordon R. Dickson

☐ DORSAI!   (#UE1342—$1.75)
☐ SOLDIER, ASK NOT   (#UE1339—$1.75)
☐ TACTICS OF MISTAKE   (#UW1279—$1.50)
☐ NECROMANCER   (#UE1353—$1.75)

The Commodore Grimes Novels of
A. Bertram Chandler

☐ THE BIG BLACK MARK   (#UW1355—$1.50)
☐ THE WAY BACK   (#UW1352—$1.50)
☐ STAR COURIER   (#UY1292—$1.25)
☐ TO KEEP THE SHIP   (#UE1385—$1.75)
☐ THE FAR TRAVELER   (#UW1444—$1.50)

The Dumarest of Terra Novels of E. C. Tubb

☐ JACK OF SWORDS   (#UY1239—$1.25)
☐ SPECTRUM OF A FORGOTTEN SUN   (#UY1265—$1.25)
☐ HAVEN OF DARKNESS   (#UY1299—$1.25)
☐ PRISON OF NIGHT   (#UW1346—$1.50)
☐ INCIDENT ON ATH   (#UW1389—$1.50)
☐ THE QUILLIAN SECTOR   (#UW1426—$1.50)

The Daedalus Novels of Brian M. Stableford

☐ THE FLORIANS   (#UY1255—$1.25)
☐ CRITICAL THRESHOLD   (#UY1282—$1.25)
☐ WILDEBLOOD'S EMPIRE   (#UW1331—$1.50)
☐ THE CITY OF THE SUN   (#UW1377—$1.50)
☐ BALANCE OF POWER   (#UE1437—$1.75)

If you wish to order these titles,

please use the coupon in

the back of this book.

Outstanding science fiction and fantasy

Presenting MICHAEL MOORCOCK
in DAW editions

The Elric Novels